The Next Time I Saw Her

The Gossamer and Pitch Trilogy: Book Two

Jae Mazer

A HellBound Books® LLC Publication

SIGN UP FOR THE HELLBOUND BOOKS NEWSLETTER:

www.hellboundbooks.com

Printed in the United States of America

Also by Jae Mazer

Novels

- Landing in Eden
- Delivery
- Pal Tailor
- Gahl's Door
- Chrysalis and Clan
- Notch (written as J.M. Adler)
- Crone: A Witch's Tale
- Beautiful Beasts: A Collection of Visceral Horror
- Ripples of Silence (co-authored with Gerry Mazer)
- Tales from the Den (co-authored with Jessica Raney)
- The Sisters Three
- Tales from Ramnon
- Mister Picket Blackmaw
- Sometimes We Don't Escape
- Salt of my Blood
- Mother Mare

Inclusion in Magazines and Anthologies:

- *The Wish* in Sicklit Magazine
- *Flight of the Crow* in Eclectically Heroic by Inklings Publishing
- *The Waif and the Witch* in Hair-Raising Tales of Villainous Confessions by Madgirl Publishing
- *Hurt* in Hair-Raising Tales of Villainous Confessions by Madgirl Publishing
- *The Ballad of Big Sammy Purdue* In Monster Party
- *Death Served* in Books of Horror Volume I
- *Of Your Own Creation* in Books of Horror Volume 2
- *Mozart in the Flames* in Books of Horror Volume 3, Part One

- *Blubber Murray* in Twisted Legends by From the Ashes Press
- *That's a Peculiar Stain on the Carpet* ... In Roadkill Texas Volume 8
- *I Didn't Hate This Goodbye* in Dead Heat: An Anthology of Summer Horror by From the Ashes Press
- *Behold, Death Arrives, A Duet of Ash and Fang* in These Lingering Shadows by Last Waltz Publishing.
- *Aisle Four* in Trapped: A Dark Dozen Anthology from Uncomfortably Dark Publishing
- *The Rise and Fall of the Corn Kings of Appalachia* in Harvested: An Anthology of Reaping What You Sow by From the Ashes Press
- *That's a Mighty Fine Head of Hair You've Got There* in Head Blown Too by Merrill David and Texas Authorcon
- *To Never Know* In Lucky Number 13 by Limitless Ink Press
- *Please* In Deviants and Decadence by Stitched Smile publishing LLC

Audioplays/Dramatizations:

Down with the Ship: Episode on July 27th, 2021 of Hearing the Haunted: A Sirenicide Production

Straight on Through: Episode on January 25th, 2021 in Hearing the Haunted: A Sirenicide Production

The Next Time I Saw Her

Chapter One

The next time I saw her, there was a man inside me. I was enjoying myself; his rhythm was perfect, his pelvis rubbed against me right where I needed it to. But my mind was elsewhere. I held onto his biceps as he thrust, feeling the strain of his muscles as he balanced above me. I breathed in, trying to smell him, smell us, but only the stemch of blood filled my nose.

And there she was, stuck up in the corner of the ceiling, licking her black lips as she watched me getting fucked.

"You okay, Anna?" the man on top of me asked.

I wasn't comfortable with the woman-thing in the corner. She was long, gangly, and naked. Her breasts were full, nipples black, and she had a bloody gash between her legs. I closed my eyes. Tried to feel the pleasure of the meat inside me. Tried to ignore the raspy cackles in the corner of the ceiling.

"Where are you?" the man asked.

His lips stopped moving. I let him deflate and slide out of me, then I rolled to the side and put my feet on the floor.

"Was it something I did?" he asked.

"No," I said, because I didn't know what else to say.

I wriggled into my jeans and slid my T-shirt over my head, all the while keeping an eye on the woman-thing attached to the ceiling like a spider. Her limbs were too long, with two elbows on each arm and two knees on each leg. Her bulbous head was perched atop a slender neck with dark purple veins pulsing beneath translucent pale skin. Her hair was long, black, and writhing. It wasn't hair. It was fine worms braided together in strands the width of a single hair. They slithered shimmering constantly in the moonlight seeping through the window.

"Are you … Are we …" The man didn't know what to say, either.

I was transfixed by the oppressive gawking of the woman thing above to help him find his words. Her lips were large, spread from ear to ear like a slash, and her mouth was a cavern with obsidian stalagmites for teeth. Her eyes were solid black, too, but in them glistened the stars like the ones over Eden's Edge—the place I had long ago fled and boxed in a deep corner of my memory.

"We're good," I said to the man.

And I left.

He didn't follow me. I hustled to the stairwell and let the heavy door slam behind me. I closed my eyes. I waited. Nothing. The woman-thing didn't chase me.

But it wasn't just a thing. She was familiar, despite the contorted bones, pallid meat, and night skies for eyes. Despite the fact that she was a grown woman with breasts and labia, I knew her. The fact that she had somehow grown a head didn't make her any less familiar to me.

"She wasn't really there," I said to the stairwell, trying to argue with my sanity about what I saw in that man's bedroom. "She isn't real."

She was then, back when I was little. Back when she had no head.

Guilt roiled in my gut about denying her existence. About forgetting our friendship.

"She was real, when she was New Friend," I clarified to the stairs, "but she's not now. Not like this. New Friend is gone, and I'm here, and everything is fine…"

The man's apartment door clicked open.

It might not be his door. It could be any door. It could be anyone. It could be him.

But I knew it wasn't, not with the clicking of her claws dragging on the ceiling behind the door, the wet rasps of breath leaking from that tear of a mouth.

No.

The door handle rattled, then creaked, slow, like a crone's wet snarl.

No!

I ran down the stairs, focusing on the slapping of my bare feet on the concrete instead of the groan of the hinges as the door opened above me. I kept going down four flights of stairs until I hit the final landing and burst into the steaming alley of Chinatown.

The city swallowed me up, sucking me from the apartment building and digesting me into its chaos. I was claustrophobic beneath the tall buildings, the bustle of people, and the ferocious glow of string and streetlights that littered the sky, murdering the stars.

I shook the hair out of my eyes and forced my feet to move. Not much was less appealing than strolling through the streets of Chinatown in bare feet, but in my haste, I had left my worn Converse in the man's apartment. That angered me more than leaving traces of my flesh on his sheets. I loved those fucking shoes.

Looky-loos gawked as I passed but basically paid me no mind. With the number of Fentanyl-filled, scantily clad street trash shambling around, I was a mere vanilla spectacle. I put distance between myself and the man's apartment, dodging questionable fluids and sharp debris as I made my way past the Gastown Steam Clock and into the Strathcona neighbourhood. It was a risky route, considering the rise in violent crime, but…

I didn't have to worry about that. Normal people had to worry about me.

Don't think about that.

My fingers cracked as I rolled them into fists, bones ready to contort, to burst through, to protect…

To destroy…

"No," I told myself and the night that lived inside me.

The dark slumbered in the marrow of my bones. It must stay there, hidden beneath layers of blood, gristle, and flesh. My trauma remained far away and long ago, right where I'd left it, ground into the dirt beneath the stars above Eden's Edge.

"I am a normal woman with a normal life," I said to the night.

Nice try, the night answered.

My breath hitched, and my stomach clenched. The voice came from in front of me. I had been so focused on the rough sidewalk beneath my bare feet that I neglected to see the figure standing in my way, just out of reach of the nearest streetlight. He was long, tall, and wide, crooked and broken. I turned away before I could read the fine lines of his features.

Without missing a beat, I spun on the balls of my feet, focusing on the pain of tearing skin as I headed back the way I had come. But my determination didn't last for long. The woman-thing was there, skittering down the pavement, head cocked to the side and arachnid limbs creeping along with a near-silent scraping.

Which direction to choose? I was in the middle of the block, so I had only two choices, unless I wanted to slink through someone's yard.

They had stopped moving, the massive man and the

arachnid woman. Were they stalking? Waiting to make a move? Or were they being gentle, allowing me time to process and calm before they engaged?

"Fuck this."

I ducked to the left, sprinting up the side of an unlit bungalow and scaling the fence, listening for all the sounds— voices, skitters, the growl of a guard dog. I wasted no time trespassing through the yard and skulked through one more yard before emerging on the next street over. I doubled back to Chinatown, where I hailed a cab. Money was tight, but the danger was suffocating. I wanted to be home safe and sound, in my apartment, in my bed, where it was quiet, and I was all alone.

Once I was in the backseat and the cab was in motion, I slipped in my AirPods and cranked up Loreena McKennitt to drown out the journey. The city lights were a serpentine, blending until I reached my apartment complex on the other side of Fraser River that bisected the city.

I paid and thanked the cabbie through the window after I slid out of the backseat; I had no interest in conversation. But it turned out I had no need to worry about small talk. Beneath his Vancouver Canucks toque, and above his flannel shirt, was a face as blank and white as fresh snow drift. With no mouth to speak, and no eyes to express emotions, there was no way for him to communicate. I thanked him again and walked inside, taking care not to glance back at the specter of my long-since-murdered father.

Chapter Two

I didn't want to wake up, but the sun poked through the blinds like fingers, prodding me into consciousness.

What would be waiting for me at the end of the bed? Teeth ready to grind my flesh, a gaping throat ready to swallow? A crooked woman ready to slice me from groin to gullet, rip out my insides, and insert herself in my meat suit to wear me, absorb me, be me.

Take me. I don't want me

Nothing was at the foot of my bed when I opened my eyes. Nothing in the corner of the ceiling or the apartment beyond the bedroom.

The clock flashed noon. I cringed. Not because I'd missed my alarm—I never set one—but because I didn't oversleep. If I had my way, I'd get out of bed right before my shift and close them right after. I only needed to be awake to exist: work, eat, pay bills, sleep. Nothing more.

I was waiting to die.

I needed coffee to start my body's engine, but I didn't think I had any left in the apartment; it had been weeks since

I last went for groceries. I mostly pecked at food at the bar during my night shift, which had gone from four days a week to seven. The owner of the Crown & Anchor, Ted, had no regard for labour laws, which worked in favour of my barren wallet. I'd started slinging drinks before I was even legal. He paid all his staff in cash and dreamed up a few extra phantom employees. That helped him cook the books, skirt time limits and hours, and all that mess. I didn't care what Ted did. My job was to pour booze, smile at sleazy humans, and wipe the slime off the bar when arms started to stick.

I was right. Not only did I not have any coffee, there was a thin layer of mold on the remaining coffee puddle at the bottom of the pot. I scolded myself and vowed to hit Save-On Foods on my way home from work.

With no coffee to drink, and my belly protesting at the thought of food, I shrugged out of my T-shirt and shorts and hopped in the shower. Cranking the water until steam rose in tendrils to the ceiling, I let the flow pelt me and imagined my skin sloughing away, revealing a new person beneath. A person who hadn't been through ten lifetimes of trauma before the age of fifteen. A person whose father wasn't a demon, and whose mother wasn't a dead witch.

I missed Mom. Deeply. With all my blood and bone and organs.

I threaded my fingers through my hair and pulled as hard as I could, summoning tears that streamed down my face and entwined with the shower water. I refused to think of Mom, of Dad, or of anything or anyone at Eden's Edge.

I pulled my hair harder.

"Stop," I yelled, angry for allowing my memories to awaken.

My mind refused to obey. Through my water-distorted vision, I saw swaths of brown fur, red feathers, and the smoke of burning buildings. I lowered my gaze to the floor of the tub, to my feet, and found the glaring yellow of Ole Man

Merle's rubber boot on my left foot. I closed my eyes, and heard the buzz of Miss Mojo's insects, the squelch of them burrowing in flesh, could feel the pierce of their stings all over my body, inside and out—

Then silence. Stillness. I couldn't hear anything, couldn't feel water.

Then a drip. And another. Droplets of water sliding off the tip of my nose and plunking on my toes. I opened my eyes to curtains of red.

The scream exploded out of my mouth, propelling a mist of blood onto the walls of my shower. Viscous crimson coated every surface, thick inside me and out. A metallic taste settled on my tongue, and globs dribbled out of my anus, my vagina, my eyes and ears and nose.

I shut off the shower streaming blood, and stepped onto my black bathmat. I knew better than to search for any colour except death. I had been down this road many times. But this blood delusion hadn't happened in years. Not since I was a teenager living on the streets, trying to blend in and be forgotten.

Toweling off was futile; I was merely smearing blood around my skin with a towel. My body wracked with violent tremors as I sobbed, and I attempted to dress myself through my fear and sorrow.

No.

I don't want this.

I want to be normal.

I want to just live.

I want to die.

And just like that, it was gone: the blood, the noise, the familiar scent of Eden's Edge.

My heart punched my ribs, the bones creaking and cracking as heat enveloped my chest before rising to my face.

I lay down on my bed, let the ceiling fan cool my skin, and took deep, measured breaths to slow my heartbeat to a manageable rate so I didn't puke or stoke out or all of the above.

I thought I had left panic attacks back in my twenties when I was self-medicating with booze, drugs, and self-harm.

Maybe these delusions won't happen again.

It's because I'm tired.

Maybe it's Covid.

I knew better.

Once I'd calmed and cooled, I resumed dressing. After donning a T-shirt and jeans, I went to slide on my shoes, forgetting that I had abandoned them the night before with the naked man in his bed with the sheets of a bachelor.

Some Cinderella, I chuckled, thinking of my dark purple Converse sitting by the door in some random dude's apartment. I couldn't remember where he lived, or what he looked like, or even what he felt like inside me. Like most times, I felt absolutely nothing. And didn't care.

I checked the clock on my microwave. Since I'd woken much earlier than I would have liked, and wasn't due at work until 4pm, I had plenty of time to swing by the mall and grab a new pair. And the mall was noisy and busy. A good distraction to keep my mind busy until my shift started to prevent the sound, sights, and smells of Eden's Edge from coming out of hiding.

Chapter Three

Pacific Center was big. Too big. I wandered aimlessly around the first floor, then the second before it occurred to me to check one of the maps for a shoe store. I should have just hit The Bay. I had wanted a distraction, but the mall was too much: the hustle and bustle of shoppers, the smell of grease traps and candied popcorn, the obnoxious buzz and flash of store lighting. Even though I had been away from living a rural life for several decades, I would never be a city girl. Give me dirt and trees over glitz and glam.

I wanted a pair of Converse, but I didn't want to wander any more to find a store that carried them. I decided to grab some food to help steady my nerves—perhaps a good portion of my mental problems were due to my steady diet of peanuts, wings, and beer. Not that mall fare was much better, but at least I'd be able to consume something green for once.

I stood in line for Teppanyaki and watched people hurry by, carrying their bags, their faces illuminated by the glow of phones held centimeters away from scrunched noses. They were missing everything. Someone could be slaughtered in the center of the food court, and no one would notice. The ones who did would see it through their phone cameras, detached, hidden behind the safety of their phone glass. Maybe it wouldn't be real, then. Maybe things don't really happen unless they happen on a screen.

"Next!"

I moved to the glass partition and ordered my meal. The cook slopped the meat and veg on the grill, flipping, scraping. The sounds were sharp nails on the insides of coffins, making my eyes water and mind buzz. I tried to focus on the din of the shoppers, but their voices escalated from conversational to feral, a chorus of angry dissonant voices drawing near, yelling. And the smell coming from the grill turned sour, the blood from the cooking meat particularly pungent. It was so gross and awful, but my mouth watered, overflowing my lips and dribbling down my chin. I wiped my face, opened my eyes, and saw the gleam of blood coating my hands.

"Ma'am?"

My jumper was soaked in blood as if my throat had been painlessly slit while I awaited my broccoli, chicken, and mini corn. And the grill was sizzling, the food screaming in pain. But it wasn't food. The globs of meat being flipped and flopped were fingers and toes, necrotic stumps covered in maggots. The cook scooped up the tainted food and put it over rice heaped in a takeaway container, giving camouflage to the maggots.

"Ma'am?"

A tap on my shoulder.

"Ma'am, your food is ready."

The man behind me had a softness in his eyes, but also maybe fear as he pointed to my takeaway container on the counter in front of me. But though his eyes were soft, his body was not. It was black muscle, hard, rippling, and shining, with an oozing obsidian cock swinging beneath his thick thighs, overtop jagged, cloven, hooves…

I took my food and ran.

I talked some sense into myself as I jogged through the mall, far away from the food court, to the tables by the Second Cup. This end of the mall was quieter. It was the intersection between The Bay and a hallway with some jewelry stores and a random shoe repair shop. I hunched over the table and opened my food, which was thankfully chicken and veg not fingers and toes. I knew that it would be, just as I knew my jumper had no blood on it, and the devil wasn't waiting back in line for his teriyaki shrimp.

It's happening again.

"No," I said to myself and to my food. "No, it isn't."

I had spells where this would happen. Hell would seep in, squirting its filth into my life, but the occurrences were few and far between. One every few years or so since leaving Eden's Edge, and mostly mild and brief. A screeching ghoul, blood on the outside of my body where it didn't belong, sounds distorted and stenches ripe. Not surprising, with my dad's demon genes speckling my blood like spots of oil.

But Mom's blood. There was no witch in my trauma. No sightings of feathers, of flowers, of bugs.

Where are you?

"No," I said. "Forget it. Forget it all."

I shoved a large crown of broccoli in my mouth and focused on the flavour, the noise of the crunch, and the ache in my jaw from struggling with a too-big bite. I could not think of such things—of the past, of what happened, of what I was.

A portly security guard whizzed by on a Segway, followed by two Mounties on foot. I chuckled. The cops were large and fit, a stark contrast to the doughy rent-a-cop who needed wheels to get around, and the three of them together were the makings of a comedy of errors. It lost its humour, though, when a third and fourth Mountie passed by at almost a run.

The entire cavalry gathered by the shoe repair shop, muttering low and close to one another. When the yellow tape came out, that's when the bystanders really took notice.

"What's going on?" the Second Cup Barista asked her co-worker, who was standing on his tippy toes, snooping over the counter for an answer.

Small clusters of shoppers began to form and more security came—Mounties, dough boys on wheels, a bulky man in a cheap suit. Pretty soon, they were herding people away from that small cul-de-sac of the mall as they cordoned off the area with their yellow tape.

I got up, left my food behind, and walked towards the chaos. As the interior of the store came into view, my heart slowed, the sound dampened, and there she was. She was behind the counter like she had any business being there, head cocked, mouth open and spilling black pitch over the counter. In her talons she held out a pair of shoes—not clean, not repaired as one would imagine a pair of shoes would be at a cobbler's shop.

But they were mine.

"You can't be here."

A Mountie stopped me, and I pointed at the shoes, *my* shoes, that were dangling from the clutches of the Corner Woman.

"My shoes," I said.

The Mountie sighed. He was about to speak, but then looked down at my feet and his mouth snapped shut. I was barefoot. In the mall.

Did I come all this way with no shoes?

Of course, I did. I had no other shoes.

"Huh," the Mountie said."

The Corner Woman dangled the shoes out like a carrot.

"Okay, Miss, which ones are they?" the Mountie asked.

"Purple Converse."

"Stay here."

The Mountie went to the store's counter where my shoes sat amongst a myriad other pairs. He went to take them but hesitated, his hand floating just overtop.

Come on, come on, come on.

I knew he shouldn't touch those shoes. Something had happened in there, and those could be evidence. But whatever had happened was in the other corner of the store, away from the rows of shoes.

How did my shoes get here?

Why?

I gasped when he picked up my shoes.

"Here," he said as he thrust them in my direction. "Now skedaddle."

And skedaddle I did. I pulled my shoes on and walked away without looking back, and without retrieving my food.

There. If you need evidence, swab those chopsticks.

I had shoes. That was my goal. A bonus was that I'd had a few mouthfuls of proper food. I ignored the fact that the shoes on my feet were actually mine, that had found their way to this mall where I just happened to be, to a crime scene where fuck knows what went down.

Don't know, don't care.

My motto since leaving Eden's Edge.

But when I placed my hand on the glass door and pushed my way out of the mall, I couldn't help but notice the fingerprints of blood I left behind. Blood that had got on my fingers from the blood-soaked backs of my purple Converse when I had pulled them on my feet.

Chapter Four

The food I'd put in my body threatened to reappear as I poured another round of Red Eyes. I was miserable and tired. The Clamato juice was stinging my fingers where I'd gnawed my fingernails pert near to the bone, and my feet were cold and wet. After I'd arrived at the bar, I washed my Converse in hot soapy water to get the blood out. It was dark and brown once it dried, so no one would have known, but I knew what it was. And I'd rather have cold wet feet than the hot reminder of blood on my skin for eight hours straight.

It was a Thursday night, so the pub was steady, but I was able to keep up with the orders just fine. Fridays and Saturdays, though we had extra staff, I was run off my feet. Most nights, the noise of the bar and its patrons grated my nerves, but tonight, it was a relief. I listened in on conversations, even joined a few. Anything to keep my mind busy. A stagnant brain was a direct route to anxiety.

At midnight, the pub decrescendoed from boisterous revelry to muffled contentment as the band broke down and people finished up the dregs of their pints. My mind was quiet, too, so I puttered about the pub, wiping tables and putting up chairs. The cooks had cleaned up and left for the night, leaving me and half a dozen stragglers behind.

"Last call, folks," I said.

The small crowd answered in groans and sass but didn't put up much of a fight. They flowed like molasses to the door, stumbling and slurring with glasses in their hands.

"Naw," I said, pointing to one customer with a large glass stein dangling loose in his grip. "I don't mind if you nip the pint glasses, but the boss'll take it out of my cheque if you leave with the good steins."

"Oops," he said. "My bad."

"No worries," I said and reached for the glass.

There was a worry, though. His boozy eyes caused him to miscalculate, and he dropped the stein before I could save it. The heavy glassware crashed to the floor, and the crowd shrieked—apologies at me and scolds at him.

"I got it," I said.

And with that, they dragged their friend out the door as he fought to stay and clean up his mess. Once they were out, I locked the door, flipped the 'open' sign to 'closed', and drew the blinds. It didn't take long to sweep up the glass and mop up the dribble of booze. There had been many a shatter and spill on these floors. One final wipe of the surfaces and I was ready to go. I grabbed a bag of trash and headed out the back door when a searing pain ripped through my hand.

"Fuck!"

That's why you put broken glass in a box, or a can, or anywhere but a flimsy kitchen trash bag. A shard of the stein had torn through the plastic and my skin as I hoisted the full bag to carry it out to the dumpster. I eyed the flaring gash on my palm while bright blood spilled down the white bag and dripped onto the clean kitchen floor.

"Fuck," I repeated as I stood there, stuck in indecision.

Clean up the garbage or clean my wound? "Fuck it."

Bleeding everywhere, I kicked my way out the back door with the garbage bag in hand. Garbage first, bloody mess later.

The alleyway was dimly lit and skittering with rats, cats, and bugs, but I was unbothered. I'd seen worse. I was bothered, however, by the stench as I approached the dumpster. It was a medley of trash, or fryer oil, and of a great many unsavory things that I couldn't distinguish from each other. I gagged while I hoisted the garbage bag with the offending glass over the side of the dumpster. It landed with a dull thud and a moan, and as I turned to walk away, anxious to escape the many odours, the trash settled and moaned again.

Moaned.

I kept my bleeding fist clenched tight and looked back at the dumpster. There was a figure perched on the top. The Corner Woman was there, her skeletal limbs twitching, her long black hair swinging in the cavern of garbage below. Her mouth gaped, wide, black, and deep enough for me to see her spine from the inside. The moan wasn't coming from her but from the dumpster.

"Hello?" I said as I hurried to the side and peered in at the piles of trash.

I didn't quite know what to expect. The Fentanyl pandemic was raging, especially in this area of Vancouver, so it wasn't unusual to find folks in a bad way on the streets, in lobbies, and even in dumpsters. And that's *almost* what this was. Inside the dumpster, buried beneath the bag I'd just tossed in, was an emaciated young man covered in filth belonging to himself and the trash. He was wearing a white tank top stained a muddy rainbow of colours, and white briefs stiff with urine and feces. But the true horror was on his face. His eyes had been gouged out, and a line had been carved from temple to temple, leaving a wound across his eyes and the bridge of his nose, exposing bone, blood, and gristle.

"Fuck, fuck," I yelled.

I crawled into the dumpster while fumbling for my phone, which I dropped into a pile of old spaghetti from the Italian restaurant next door.

"Help!" I called towards the street while I took the man's hand. "It's okay," I said softly in his ear. "I'm here."

He was jibbering something resembling words. Drool poured from his mouth. He soiled himself again, his urine warm against my leg while I tried to calm him and stay calm myself. A couple people came running to my cries, someone called 9-1-1, while other voices barked commands.

"Leave him there!"

"Pull him out."

"Don't touch him!"

"What happened?"

"His face, his face, his face…"

I stayed there, holding his hand, touching his cheek, speaking soft comforts to him as his skin grew colder, his breath hitched in his chest, and he rattled out the final wheeze, welcoming death. He was gone before the alleyway lit with red and blue, a spastic frenzy of emergency lights and a song of voices full of urgency and procedure.

The paramedics took me out of the dumpster first and wrapped me in a blanket. I suppose the dumpster man had no need of a blanket. Not anymore. They didn't lift him out right away. Not while I was there. They marked off the scene with yellow tape, and I wondered if it was the same roll of yellow tape they used at the mall. They asked if I was hurt, and I said no. They pointed to my bloody palm, and I told them what I was.

I'm a witch. And a demon. My mother was a witch, my father was a demon, and they loved each other, fucked, and made me, and we all loved each other until I murdered him, and we moved away, and everyone died.

"A bartender?" the officer confirmed.

"Yes."

This officer was firm, but he wasn't intimidating or mean. Just to the point and neutral.

"You cut yourself on a broken glass?" he asked.

I nodded.

"Can anyone confirm this?"

Another nod. "The customer who broke it, maybe."

"He saw you cut yourself?"

I shook my head. "But we have cameras. And there's probably blood."

I nodded towards the back door of the pub.

"And on the garbage bag," I said, tilting my chin at the dumpster.

"Your blood will be in there, too?" the officer asked, his eyebrows scrunched together like an accusatory mustache atop a frowning lip.

"Yes," I confirmed.

"With his."

"Yes. There is plenty of blood in there, I'm sure. Among other things."

"Other things?"

"Smell for yourself."

The officer paused a beat before scribbling something on his notepad. He was a beautiful man. His clothes were clean, his face smooth and dark, his hair full and shiny.

"Was he like that when you found him?" he asked.

"Dead?"

"Mutilated."

"Yes." I took a deep breath, trying not to taste the garbage on my tongue.

My eyes caught movement from above. The Corner Woman was still sitting on the dumpster, crouched, her bloody gash splayed open, its juices shining beneath the lights the crime scene investigators had set up. She was watching me, trilling soft notes from her throat, clicking her nails on the steel of the dumpster lid.

"His eyes were… He was still alive, though. He made a noise when I threw the garbage bag in."

"The one with the broken glass."

"Yes. And he made the noise again. That's when I found him."

"And you climbed in?"

"Of course, I fucking did. He needed help. He needed…"

Someone to comfort him, be with him as he passed.

He was all alone.

Like me.

My stomach roiled. I belched, and the taste of teriyaki bubbled in my throat. Heat flushed through my body, then cold as tiny black stars started twinkling in my vision. The Corner Woman stood, balanced and gripping onto the dumpster lip with her foot talons, and cawed a shrill keen towards the paramedics. They didn't startle, but one did glance at the beautiful officer and me. It wasn't long before he was at my side.

"Sir, let me do my job, please," the paramedic said.

"What?" the officer said. "I'm right in the middle of—"

"She's in shock," the paramedic said as he wrapped his arm around me. "And she might pass—"

Blackness. But even in the dark nothingness I could feel the Corner Woman holding my hand and easing me into a peaceful unconsciousness.

Chapter Five

There was nothing wrong with me. Nothing they could see, anyway. After I passed out, they'd taken me to the hospital and run the mandatory tests to see if there was anything fucked up in my body or head, or if I had any injuries beyond the cut on my palm. After they were satisfied that I wasn't seriously injured or ill, they cleaned and dressed my wound and hurried me out the door.

Unfortunately for the taxi driver, they hadn't allowed me to shower. I was covered in a three-course meal of cold spaghetti sauce, urine, and blood.

"Been through the wringer, eh?" the driver asked.

"Something like that."

He rolled down his window, trying to get some fresh air, I assumed. I couldn't tell which was worse. The stench of rot and death on me or the belch-breaths of diesel, gas, and city life lingering outside the cab like a fog.

By the time I got home, the sun was already awake. I wasn't ready for the light. I closed myself in my apartment, made sure the blinds were drawn tight, and downed two full glasses of ice-cold water. Despite having an IV at the hospital, I was parched, and my mouth tasted and felt like I'd consumed steaming rat shit. When I passed my hall mirror en-route to my shower, I had a good look at myself. My clothes were stiff and stained, and my hair was mangled like a birch broom in the fits. Deciding that cleaning my clothes was a waste of energy, I stripped naked and tossed them in a trash bag. All except my purple Converse, which I placed into the kitchen sink to soak in some hot water and Oxyclean.

The shower was orgasmic. I let the water run over me for several minutes as it heated to scorching, then I scrubbed my skin raw to wash away any evidence of what had happened over the past few days…

…My whole damn life…

…And once I was clean, I let the conditioner sit in my hair while I brushed my teeth at the bathroom sink.

My shower curtain squeaked behind me. My first instinct was to reach for a towel, like the main concern was the shame of my nudity and not the potential murderer in my apartment. As I grasped onto the towel hanging off the hook on the door, the squeak came again. It wasn't the shower curtain, which hung there unmoving, but something behind it. Small and quiet, as if barely there.

I covered myself in the towel and drew back the curtain.

It was a squirrel, plump and fluffy, sitting in the bottom of the bathtub, wringing his little hands, his bushy red tail coiled. I froze, staring into his beady black eyes as his nose twitched and teeth chittered. I refused to believe what I was seeing.

Get out, I said, but the words didn't come out of my mouth. Didn't matter. I knew he could hear me.

Why are you here, Gus?

I don't want you here.

I don't want any of this. Not anymore.

I wasn't convinced I wanted him gone. I let the towel drop

to the floor and got into the tub. He waited until I was still and crawled up my leg, across my stomach, and settled in between my breasts with his tail wrapped around himself like a shawl.

"Oh, Gus," I said as I scratched the fur behind his ears. "I missed you."

I hadn't seen my familiar since I'd left Eden's Edge. The memories of Gus weren't bad per se, but other memories clung to his fur like shit. Memories of pain and death, torture and murder. I wished none of it had ever happened. I wished I had my mom, and we lived in a cottage in the woods, and that I never saw headless girls and ghosts of fisherman and that I was a normal woman with a normal life…

I stroked Gus's fur. I didn't know much about witchcraft still. I knew a bit—what my mother had shown me, what Miss Mojo had told me, and what I had read in books. But I'd never had the chance to practice and experiment. Gus came from me. Rebirthed from my very womb. My familiar.

I wondered if the reverse would work to undo what had been done.

"I love you," I said to Gus, because I did. I truly did, but I wanted him gone. I wanted that part of me gone.

I gave Gus a little hug and smooch on the nose, then turned the faucet on and grabbed a bottle of conditioner. He leaned into my touch and I massaged the cream into her fur, slathering him until he was smooth and soft. I scooped him up in my hands, let my knees fall open until they touched the sides of the tub, and moved him down between my legs.

Gus did not prefer this plan. As I spread my vulva and began to work him inside, he fought me, wriggling and trying to get away. I held him tight, which was no small feat with how greasy the conditioner was. I shoved him face first inside of me. A few centimeters in, he panicked and started clawing and biting. I felt bad for him. Poor little dude couldn't breathe, but this had to be done, and I had to hurry before the white-hot pain caused my grip to falter, giving Gus the opportunity to escape.

I started cramming him in violently and felt his tiny bones snap against the inner walls of my vagina. I shoved, pushed, and poked until he was deep inside, then I took a slender shampoo bottle and jammed him in deep as he could go. The bath was now half-full of a slurry of water, fur, blood, and flesh. I let the water run, slid lower, squeezed my knees together, and held onto my throbbing abdomen while Gus thrashed and mewled inside me. When the water was deep enough to submerge nearly all of me, save my face, and my feet which were up on the wall, I closed the faucet and soaked with water in my ears and pain in my guts.

Gus didn't settle until dark hair tickled my belly. Corner Woman was hanging from the ceiling, her hair draped over my naked body, her eyes wide and watching. She placed a long, taloned hand on my tummy until Gus quieted and finally fell still. I stayed that way for the longest time, drifting in and out of consciousness as trees and graves, squirrels and red birds waltzed through my dreams.

Chapter Six

I had quite the mess to clean up in the morning. I woke in the tub, surprised (and somewhat disappointed) that I didn't drown. It took almost a full hour to clean up the blood and hair that filled the tub, and even longer to tend to myself. The insides of my thighs were shredded from Gus's thrashing; I didn't even want to think about how it looked up inside me. I took a hot shower then disinfected the visible wounds before bandaging what I could, putting on a pad, and finding thick, soft pants that would be gentle to the damage.

I didn't check my phone. I wondered what work would say about the events of the previous night, but I also didn't want to deal with any of that. Not just yet.

What I did need to deal with was groceries. I had to eat, and mall and bar food wasn't going to cut it. I usually shopped on Fridays because it was the quietest day of the week to go. So, I tossed on a jumper, pulled on my Converse, and headed to Save-on Foods. If I had a car, I could have just ordered groceries and picked them up without ever having to grace the inside of the store, but it felt good to move. What didn't feel good was seeing police cars at the side of the grocery store, clustered around like hyenas circling a kill.

I ignored it, parked on the opposite side of the lot, and went inside. I was laser focused—the same old list in my same old brain.

- o Frozen dinners
- o Berries
- o Tea
- o Coffee Crisp

And I added another item that I figured I might need for the week.

- o Adult diapers.

The stinging and burning in my nether regions was intense. Gus had left quite the massacre down under, and I was soaking through a pad every twenty minutes. Part of me wondered if I should go see a doctor, if I was at risk of bleeding out or infection. But the sensible part of me knew that jamming a squirrel up my pussy, whether it was magical or not, would land me directly in the loony bin. And as nice a break as that might have been, I had bills to pay and no one to help me. I couldn't be homeless. Not again.

With my trolly full and me anxious to get out, I stood in line, waiting for the old woman in front of me to load her plethora of groceries onto the belt. She looked to be about 284 years old, and had the coordination of an intoxicated sloth, so watching her take one can at a time, put it on the belt, then rearrange it twice before moving on to the next item was enough to drive me mad. To save my sanity and prevent an outburst, I glanced around the store to find soothing sights to fixate on.

I found something worse. The detective from the night before—the one who had interviewed me—was hovering by the exit doors, notepad in hand, interviewing a store employee and a guy in a white button-down shirt who must have been the store manager. The employee was visibly shaken—grey skin, trembling hands, biting his lower lip. He was just a boy—couldn't have been more than fifteen years old. But it appeared whatever happened would age him real quick.

I didn't want to find out. I checked back at the ancient crone, who was now flipping open her chequebook and fumbling through her massive pocketbook for a pen.

"Hurry up," I muttered under my breath.

The old timer didn't hear, but the cashier sure did. The young woman gave me a shrug and a smirk. What are you gonna do?

I debated about leaving all my groceries behind. I could eat at the bar. We had garnish that was green, mixers with vitamin C, and appetizers I might be able to snatch before they got dipped in the deep fryer.

I dared to look back at the trio of terror—the detective, the shuddering employee, and the blustering manager. The employee was crying now, the manager was puffing his chest at the detective, and the detective's jaw was set firm, his stance wide, his notepad closed. He was done. Either he was about to make an arrest, or he was posturing for the two men—one scared, one aggressive—to make an inappropriate move.

"Ma'am?"

The old bitch was gone, and the cashier had already rung up my items. Now it was me holding up the line. I stuttered an apology to the people behind me, paid, and headed towards the exit with my head down. There were many people moving through the exit, so I joined the swarm with my hood up, hoping to pass by the commotion unnoticed. And I was just about in the clear, too. My feet hit the pavement outside when the voice came at me from behind.

"Seems trouble has a way of finding you," he said.

I stopped. To keep walking would be to admit guilt, and I had nothing to be guilty about. But I was nervous just the same.

"Hello, Detective," I said and faced him. "Fancy meeting you here."

"You didn't get much rest last night," he noticed, his gaze fondling me from head to toe.

No, sir, I did not. I was re-inserting a squirrel into my womb. And sleeping in a bathtub full of blood is mighty uncomfortable.

"I never sleep well." That was true. My fingers twitched to rub my temple like that would ease my exhaustion.

"The name's Detective Hill. Call me Kaz, though."

"Kaz?" I asked, trying to school my features. First name basis?

"Yeah." He studied my face as if it could reveal all my secrets.

I expected him to take out his notebook, to cuff me, something.

"You seem nervous," he said, gesturing to my stiff shoulders with his pen.

"I am," I said.

"Why?" He scribbled something in his notebook.

"Police make me nervous. I haven't had many dealings with them, except…" I didn't want to explain. I didn't know how.

"You have a record?" he asked, pausing his pen.

I shook my head. "Foster care. Since I was real young."

His expression softened. "Ah," he said. "Well, Anna— Is it okay if I call you Anna?"

I nodded. That's my name, so what else would he call me?

"Anna, I'm just trying to put two and two together. We have no shortage of crime around here, but two deaths in proximity… Something smells fishy, and this body's not in a dumpster."

The slight tensing of his lips told me that he wanted to chuckle. But this was not a tasteless man, or a mean one, so he held back the crude humor.

He probably laughs and jokes when he's uncomfortable. I do that all the time.

"Another death?" I asked.

I looked over his shoulder at the corner of the building, where the gaggle of officers had taped it up like Christmas and were swarming about like worker ants, heads down, all business.

"Indulge me," Kaz said.

He walked towards the scene, and with a nod, beckoned me to come. I was going to ask if I should come, if I should be this close to a crime scene when I wasn't authorized, but Kaz was taking me there. He was a cop, and judging by his suit and demeanor, I think he was higher up on the food chain as far as cops went. So, I followed, a puppy with my tail between my legs being led to the urine I'd left on the carpet.

He stopped at the narrow mouth of the service road that led alongside the grocery store and held up the crime scene tape for me to pass beneath. There was a screen erected to block people from peeking in from the parking lot, but he pulled that back, too, and led me around to the other side.

It was worse than puppy urine. So much worse.

There was a body on the ground. It wasn't covered by a sheet; I suppose it didn't have to be, not with the screen blocking the view. This body was different from the one I'd found in the dumpster the night before. It was a woman: curvaceous, wearing expensive clothes, and her nails precisely manicured into pale pink coffins. Though stained with blood, her hair was a perfect ash blonde, a colour that would take expensive amounts of bleach and toner to attain.

She was no fentanyl addict like the boy in the dumpster. She wasn't poor, or sick, or male. But there was something identical about them.

I wondered what colour her eyes would have been if they were still in her head.

"Familiar?" Kaz asked.

Were they pale blue like an iceberg? Or green like the waters in Banff National Park? Brown like the earth back at Eden's Edge…

"Anna." Kaz took a hold of my arm. Gentle, though. He wasn't mad.

I couldn't look away from the body, but I knew he was watching my every move, my reactions, and my expressions. "It's …" I couldn't find words.

Awful? Yes. Horrible? Yeah. A weird coincidence? So much more than that.

"You recognise that?" he asked.

I couldn't look at him. I had a hard enough time tearing my gaze from the victim on the ground, but I did look up when he pointed a finger right across my line of sight. I followed that finger to the side of the grocery store, and the artwork painted on the brick in blood.

It was a trio of hearts, two big ones on the outside and a little one in the middle. They were all squished together, blood drooling down as if the hearts were real and being squeezed by phantom hands.

"Have you seen this before?" Kaz asked.

Yes. "No," I lied.

"Maybe at the pub?" he asked.

"No," I said, and this time it was the truth.

The last time I saw this design, it was finger painted on a window of a diner in the middle of nowhere, right after I'd murdered my dad and mom, and I was on the run. A little girl I'd just met at that diner had painted it. She had such a beautiful dress, and shiny black shoes, and no head. I thought of New Friend, of how she'd cared for me at Eden's Edge before I razed it to the ground.

I thought of her now, no longer a little girl, no longer headless, reappearing so far from that diner and those woods, all these years later. She looked nothing like she once had, but I supposed I was different, too.

I looked at the wall above the victim.

Hello, Friend, I thought at her. Because she was no longer new.

She was a crooked, impossible thing latched onto the side of that grocery store like a spider, her long hair sticking to the bloody design she'd finger painted onto the brick with those necrotic fingers of hers. I didn't know it when she was in that bedroom, hanging high in that corner and watching me get fucked. But I knew it now, just as I know my very own flesh. It was her. New Friend. Or just Friend, rather. She'd come to me.

I couldn't help but smile. So many times I'd imagined her with a head, wondered what colour her hair might be and how she'd had it cut. I'm sure it would have been beautiful if it wasn't long, matted, and soaked in blood.

Is it black? Brown? Maybe even blonde?

"Something amusing?" Kaz asked.

Friend's head whipped towards him, and a baritone growl rumbled from her belly.

"I laugh when I'm nervous." I looked at him this time, directly in the eye, squaring my shoulders.

Mom's voice chimed in my ear. *"We are smart. We are strong. Be strong."*

"What is all this?" I asked Kaz, waving my hand over the crime scene. "What does this have to do with me?"

"You tell me," he said.

"How would I know?" I asked.

"Thoughts?" he asked.

"I'm not a detective, so…" I said.

"You are the only witness thus far. Poor bloke came out to the loading dock and found her here like this, dead already, the Picasso already smeared on the wall. Yours was alive when you found him."

"No artwork, though," I said, staring at the wall where

Friend was still hanging, retracing her painted lines with her middle finger.

"But also, no eyes," Kaz said, motioning to the woman on the ground and her emptied sockets. "And you just happen to be here, too."

"I require food," I said. "To live."

A sneaky smirk teased the corners of his mouth.

"The pub isn't far from here," I said. "Everything's within walking distance. The places I go, I mean. I don't drive. This store is close."

He nodded, then redirected his attention back to the crime scene. "Yeah," he said. "Just trying to figure it all out."

"Are there others?" I asked. "Like this?"

"Not that we know of. Just last night, and now this."

"How long has she been here?" I asked.

"Couldn't have been long," he said. "Someone would've found her pretty quick."

"But long enough to do that," I said, pointing at the art on the wall.

"Listen," he said. "I have your number. I'll give you a ring if I need you, or if something else comes up. I may want to interview you again."

"No problem," I said.

He held my gaze for a moment before motioning for me to get the fuck out of the crime scene. I went, taking care not to hurry because speed could mean guilt, but also because I wanted to glance back and gaze into the eyes of my long-lost friend.

I've missed you, I thought at her.

Her cavernous maw twisted into a smile as a thick, clotted, bloody tear trickled down her grey cheek.

Chapter Seven

It was a gossip factory at work that night. A full assembly line of questions and nervous looks from nosy nellies awaited me as soon as I stepped foot in the pub. I made sure to arrive fifteen minutes late—which I never do—to avoid having to use the back entrance before the front door was unlocked. I had no desire to be in that alleyway again. Not yet, not where a life had ended, and the smell of blood remained. So, I strolled in the front door after the place was open, hoping that my tardiness would also not allow for questions before the customers started filtering in. But gossip waits for no business.

"What was it like?" Sheila asked before she even attended to her first table.

"You should get them," I said, pointing at the couple in the booth.

"Were you freaked the fuck out?" she asked.

"Of course, I fucking was."

I walked into the kitchen to grab an apron I never wore, just to get away from Shitty Sheila and her nonsense.

Unfortunately, Robbie was there, heating up the oil in the deep fryer and chopping the parsley for garnish. Sheila was bad, but Robbie survived on a steady diet of chicken wings and other people's drama.

"You tossing your kills in our dumpster?" he said, then let out a series of cough-laughs that sprayed over the food and surfaces.

This is why I need to eat my own groceries.

"He was there before I got there," I said as I sifted through the aprons, trying to find one without stains and filth.

"'Nother junkie, I suppose," Robbie said.

"Think so," I said. "But that's not why he died."

Robbie put down his chopping knife.

Oh fuck.

"Was there blood?" Robbie asked.

"Robbie—" I stared.

"Guts? Was he in pain?" Robbie asked.

"Of course he was in pain, you fuckwad. He had his eyes scooped out of his skull while he was still alive, so…" I said.

The glee on Robbie's face was akin to a child receiving a pony on Christmas Day. I'd just fed this drama junkie the equivalent of an eight-ball of information.

"I literally just came in my pants," he said.

"Oi, fuck right off," I said.

"It's dribbling into my Crocs right now. Tell me more."

"Ugggghhhhhhh."

I gave up on my apron hunt, which was just a reason to avoid Sheila anyway, and headed back out to behind the bar where I belonged.

As per usual, Saturday night was slammed. A steady of flow of customers wandered in until it was shoulder-to-shoulder people filling the pub. We had a live musician playing, whose gentle folk rock was barely audible over the roar of the crowd—clinking glasses, laughter, fights, and flirtation. A little bit of everything mixed into an ear-splitting medley of white noise. By midnight, my head was pounding, my mouth was dry from anxiety and stress, and my muscles ached. I was almost tempted to take five to stand in the alleyway where it would be dark and quiet.

Almost.

The overdosing of noise, movement, and smells were more appealing than being back at the dumpster where whatever happened had happened.

By one in the morning, I was rethinking my decision. I was ready to not only go out to that dumpster, but to crawl inside and shut the lid. And now, on top of it all, my stomach was roiling. I was hungry, but also cramping, and the noise of my guts gurgling and churning contributed to the cacophony. After every few drinks I poured, I stopped to catch my breath. The pain finally became so intense that I was bent over and couldn't reach for the bottles from the top shelf.

Sheila put her hand on my back. "Girl, the fuck?"

"Period," I said. I couldn't get much more out.

"That's a pretty bad one," Sheila said. "You sure that's all?"

I was sure. I was sure it wasn't my period. I was cold, but beaded sweat on my forehead pooled together to form creeks that ran down my nose and dripped to the floor.

"I think I need a minute," I said.

I didn't wait for a response. I passed through the kitchen, ignoring Robbie's bitching about maggots in the Brussel sprouts, and burst into the alleyway. The cool air hit me like a wall, as did the silence, and my stomach immediately calmed.

"Okay," I said. "Okay."

I walked a few paces towards the mouth of the alley, away from the murder dumpster, and slid down the wall until I was seated on the pavement in a puddle of grime and muck. I didn't care. I felt awful, and I needed to sit and calm my nerves and stomach. I wish I'd grabbed some water on the way out, but I didn't want to pause in that kitchen for fear I'd pass out, throw up, or worse.

I closed my eyes and focused on my breathing, just like Mom taught me. The cool air was refreshing, even though it smelled like a urinal in the alleyway—a urinal mixed with pints of blood. But I tried to ignore that, tried to slow my breathing and mind.

A burst of pain torqued my stomach, and a silent scream escaped my mouth as I crunched into a ball and rolled onto my side. Frantically, I unbuttoned my jeans to relieve the pressure, but it was no help. A warm gush of fluid soaked the denim, and through the all-encompassing pain, I couldn't tell whether I had pissed or shit myself; the alleyway reeked of both.

I managed to get to my hands and knees and crawl behind the dumpster for some privacy so I could shed my jeans all together. With those off, I had some relief, but it still felt like there was a fist inside me, clenching tight to my colon, intestines, and womb, and braiding the three together with force. I laid on my back with my feet in the air, then on my stomach, then on my left side and brought my knees to my chest. I did everything people were supposed to do when suffering with any kind of gastrointestinal ailment, but nothing would relieve the pain.

"Pusssshhhhhhh."

Friend was there, perched on her haunches atop the dumpster, looking at me.

"No fucking way," I growled through gritted teeth. "He's staying in there."

"Pussssssshhhhhhhh."

Friend's hair draped over my belly and my soaked panties and snaked down my legs like veins. With her feet curled on the dumpster, she lowered her upper half until she was on her elbows between my legs, forcing my knees apart.

"No," I screamed.

But as I unleashed the word, something squiggled up inside me. I held my hands over my exits and slammed my knees back together. Friend retreated, sat on the dumpster, and allowed me to suffer. I bit my fist, and used every muscle to hold in that furry little fucker. He crowned, his wet nose twitching and sniffling against my hands, and I shoved him back in as deep as I could.

The breaking of glass from the other side of the dumpster caught my attention. I held my breath and tried to stop moving.

No one can find me like this.

Thankfully, Gus quieted, too. He stilled inside me, retreating deeper, and the pain subsided enough for me to be breathe and relax. Footsteps were approaching, crunching over broken glass, slow and hard. And there was something else; a hissing like a leaking balloon. There were other sounds—the music from inside the pub, conversations from the street, the whoosh of cars on the pavement—but these sounds faded to silence, amplifying the footsteps and the hissing.

I wanted to run but wasn't confident I could get to my feet, let alone move fast enough to escape whatever was creating the noise. Besides, I was in my panties, so bursting back into the pub was a horrible option.

The footsteps were approaching in slow motion, pounding the pavement, clopping…

…Hooves…

…And decreasing in speed as they drew near. The hissing was speckled with the sniffing of an animal, and I wondered how many somethings were coming for me, or if it was a single, terrible creature that both hissed and sniffed, walked and clopped.

Friend was looking at the alley, her many rows of teeth bared, her long talons tensed to slash. She was my eyes, so I watched her, and with every step The Something took, she rose a few more centimeters until she was standing tall, balanced on the edge of the dumpster, looming over what lurked below.

I knew The Something had reached the dumpster at the scrape of nails on the rusted metal. A few scrapes and taps, then the entire dumpster shifted, rolling back.

It's going to crush me!

There was no room for me to hide underneath, and I had no time to dress myself before running into the restaurant, but I decided to make a move for shame and go inside anyway. Robbie would get a thrill, and Sheila would have plenty to talk about, but I would be away from this Something that seemed so intent on paying me a visit.

Once I was committed, I didn't hesitate. I launched to my feet and ran, aiming for the door. I didn't look at what awaited me on the other side of the dumpster. I grabbed ahold of the door handle and yanked it.

Locked.

"I didn't lock it," I said to the door. "I didn't lock you!"

Clip. Clop. Clip. Clop.

I didn't turn. The Something was there, breathing on my neck, its breath thick and hot.

Dad. It's only the Blankness. The demon that is my father that visited me in Eden's Edge.

I expected a long, tall man with no face, a bowler hat, and a glowing name badge.

But it wasn't Dad.

My face was mere centimeters from the abdomen of something completely…wrong. I had seen many a monster, but this wasn't just any monster. The Wrong was evil incarnate, a rancid thing constructed of pain and gore. It was twice my height and four times my width—not obese, but a mass of solid muscle. It had obsidian flesh pocked with oozing sores and curled horns that stabbed into its own temples. Its eyes were screens upon which played the most horrid moments of my life; the death of my dad, mom, and friends, played over and over in its television eyes like a glitching VHS tape. Its mouth was full of grave dirt and horn worms that spilled out every time it worked its jaw like it was trying to speak. But there were no words, only the distant screams of tortures echoing up its throat like the damned resided in this thing's bloated belly.

I regretted looking down. That bloated belly sat like a shelf atop The Wrong's genitals that were engorged, throbbing, abnormal. It had not one cock, but four. One hung there like it should—large, limp and swinging between its knees. Two cocks were raised and swaying like cobras on either side of The Wrong, and the final cock was erect and plunged deep into the beast's rectum.

"No," I said as one of the snake cocks crept up and brushed my cheek.

"No," I repeated when the other one sniffed my ribs, down my stomach to my panties where Gus had resumed his struggle to claw his way free.

This time I let him.

He burst forth from my vagina with a gush of blood and fluid, then wrangled around in my panties until he found his way out. Friend already had her talons around one of the snake cocks while Gus sank his teeth into the other one, chomping off a chunk of meat before going in for a second taste. The Wrong stumbled back but looked more irritated than in pain. He swiped at Friend and Gus, but they came back for more, giving me a chance to once again place my hand on the door handle that I was so sure I hadn't locked.

This time, it opened freely.

I stumbled inside, shut and locked the door for real this time, then staggered towards the bathroom behind the kitchen. I didn't make it. As the floor rushed at me, my bright vision melding with the white tile that received my face with a smack, Robbie's Crocs squeaked as he ran to my side, abandoning his worm-riddled Brussel sprouts to come to my aid.

Chapter Eight

It wasn't the incessant beeping of machines and monitors that told me I was in a hospital. It was that smell—a medley of alcohol swabs, sick, latex, and blood.

I hated hospitals.

They were never a problem when I was little. Mom took me to my regular doctor's appointments and into urgent care when I got strep throat, or when I broke a bone playing too hard. Doctors were always nice, nurses were efficient and knowledgeable, and nothing so bad as serious illness or death had befallen me or my folks. All that nonsense happened in the wild, mostly by my hands.

"Anna?"

This nurse was young, likely younger than me from the look of it. My youth was escaping quietly while I wasn't paying attention. Last I'd thought of my age, I was thirty-odd years old. I didn't celebrate birthdays. I didn't bother to keep track. My eyes fluttered open, and I took in my surroundings—a private room. A glance out the window—on the fourth floor, I'd guess. Vancouver General, probably.

"How are you feeling?" the nurse asked.

Like I've just given birth.

"Sore," I said.

The young nurse pressed my call button.

What is that for?

An officer came into the room.

Oh.

"Let's wait for the doctor," the nurse said to the male cop.

The officers disregarded her. The male cop stood back while the female stepped forward and sat on the bed. Her weight compressed the plastic mattress and rolled me against her. I winced.

"Don't do that," the nurse said and grabbed for the cop's arm.

The male cop placed his palm on his weapon. The female cop stood, and the bed swelled back into place.

"Sorry," the nurse said as she flashed both cops a glare. "Never touch a victim, please."

"Victim?" I said.

I tried to scooch myself into a seated position, forgetting where I was. The nurse stopped me and raised the head of the bed with the push of a button. Good thing. My stomach muscles were spent.

"Anna?" the female cop said. "I'm Detective Empusa. Do you know why you're here?"

Detective Empusa didn't introduce her male counterpart, which means they think I was raped.

I assure you, nothing went in there. But something did come out.

I wondered where Gus was now and what he was up to.

"I got sick at work," I said, which was true.

"You were attacked," Empusa said.

"How so?"

I realized both my question and my tone were a tad harsh by the look of shock on their faces. But Empusa wasn't deterred.

"What's the last thing you remember?" Empusa asked.

"Passing out on the floor of the kitchen at The Crown and Anchor."

"Before that?"

I was in the alley parlaying with a four-cocked demon. But don't worry. My squirrel familiar and my imaginary friend fought him off so I could get away.

"I went out to the dumpster to get some fresh air," I said.

"The dumpster," she said.

"Yes," I confirmed.

"For fresh air," she stated. Questioning.

"Not right inside it," I said. "Just needed to go outside."

She was scratching away on her notepad. The noise seemed much louder than it should have, and the hospital smells were making my stomach roil. And one of the officers—either He-cop or She-cop—had profound body odour. Almost gamey.

"What time did you arrive on shift?" Empusa asked.

"Four-ish. No wait. Closer to half-past," I said.

"Why were you late?" Empusa asked.

"Because I wanted to be," I said, no small amount of snark in my tone.

Empusa's gaze lifted from her notebook and met mine.

"I had trouble the night before," I said. "Out in the alley. I wanted to come through the front door, which doesn't open until four."

"Trouble?"

"There should be a police report."

"Can *you* tell me?"

I looked at her, at her shit-brown eyes and mousey hair tied in a tight plait. Her partner was slightly overweight, and his breathing whistled through congestion in his sinuses, despite his mouth gaping below a gross, greasy mustache.

"I cannot," I said.

"Why not?"

"DEN THA," I shouted. "I WILL NOT."

The words thundered out of my throat in voices that didn't belong to me. Baritones swirled with altos mixed with a soprano. My defiance shocked me, as did the impossible voice and language that came from my body.

Empusa stared at me for a moment before the scratching began again.

"What the fuck are you writing?" My hand flew over my mouth. My inside voice had never ventured outside before.

Empusa stopped writing, and her hand curled around her pen like she brandished it like a weapon. Her teeth ground together, the muscles in her jaw working as she bit down in anger.

"That's enough," the young nurse said. "She's been through enough, and—"

"You've been raped," Empusa said.

"I haven't," I argued.

"You have. Your co-worker found you in bloody panties with claw marks on the insides of your thighs."

Again, I spoke in a myriad tones at a volume that didn't belong in such an enclosed space. "Robbie Cum Crocs has no business with his face between my thighs."

I harked up a wad of blood and spit it down on the sheets overtop the 'Y' of my groin.

"It's like I'm on the bloody rag!" I laughed. Shock stole my breath like a punch to the guts. "I'm so sorry," I said. My voice was soft again. Mine. I had control of my functions. "I'm unwell," I explained. "I mean, I haven't been feeling great. Long hours, not eating right, all that."

I'm possessed.

Empusa loosened her jaw to continue her questioning. "Have you been having difficulties with anyone at work? Customers, this Robbie…Cum Crocs?"

I would have laughed if I'd been in a laughing mood.

"No," I said. "He and I are good. And no, no problematic patrons, either."

"Roofies are an issue right now," Empusa said. "We'd like to run a tox screen."

"Of course."

Her voice softened, though I could tell it was by force. This was not a soft woman.

"And a rape kit. It'll be quick, and only myself and the doctor will be in the room—"

"No."

They weren't looking inside me. I knew what they would find—scratches, bites, and roan fur. Perhaps a nut or two.

"I know you're upset," Empusa said, "and it's been a hard few hours, but—"

"ÓCHI."

This time, the word burst from me with a mist of crimson that hung in the air like smog. I followed it up with a gut-deep belch, then a spew of vomit raced up my esophagus. I put my hand over my mouth to dam it, but there was no stopping the geyser of bile that poured over my chest and all over the bedclothes.

"That's enough," the young nurse barked, sounding every bit as terrifying as my foreign voices did. "Out!"

The officers obeyed. Though I suspect they just wanted to get away from my rantings and my steaming vomit. I knew they were going to wait around, though. They had to stay, to get their evidence, to complete their report. And the longer I made them wait, the more irritated they'd get. Even after only knowing her for a few short minutes, patience and kindness weren't skills in her repertoire. What a strange bird to assign to a rape case.

And she walked funny. As she headed out the door, her gait was...off. Uneven, a defined limp, the step of her left foot slightly heavier than her left.

Everything was so weird. There were insects framing my

vision, thousands of fluttering wings, probiscis tongues, wispy legs. I turned my head to see, but they flitted away as if terrified of my glance. My blood flow felt like maggots surfing my blood stream, millepedes gyrating in my bowels. My mouth tasted of dirt and blood, and everything stank of death.

"I wasn't raped," I told the young nurse once we were alone behind closed doors.

"You can see why they'd think that, yes? With the injuries."

"Suppose so."

"I could understand rough sex, role-plays, all that jazz, but you stumbled in from your work break incoherent in a pair of bloodied-up panties. You see how that comes across."

"Yeah."

"But let's not worry about that now. Let's get you and this bed cleaned up."

She guided me to my feet and braced me until I had my balance. Still unconvinced I wouldn't topple; she walked me over to the little couch by the window before stripping the bed.

"I'm so sorry," I said as she balled up the soiled sheets. "I don't know what... I don't feel sick."

But there was a sickness inside of me. Something tainted and wrong.

"Oh, that's no mind," she said with a smile. "Honestly, I got more wigged out by that rank body odour of theirs."

Now I laughed. I couldn't help it, and she laughed too as she waved her gloved hand in front of her face. It felt so good to share this humor with someone, that my chuckles turned to tears, and I cried and laughed and cried some more while the young nurse abandoned the sheets to come sit with me and hold my hand. We were like that for a few minutes before her cellphone chimed an alert.

"Go ahead," I said. "It might be HazMat wondering if

there's a chemical leak in this room."

The laughter ignited again, and she pulled her phone out of the pocket of her scrubs. But her humour faded when she read what was on the screen.

"Anna, do you have anyone who could come and help you?"

The question startled me out of my giggles. I had an answer. I didn't even have to think about it, but I hesitated. I had never really admitted it aloud.

"No," I said, and tears burned my eyes again, threatening to take center stage. "My family is…gone, and I don't have any friends."

"Any?"

I shook my head.

Pathetic.

The voice inside my head was thick and low, like it existed in a glob of mucus. I didn't recognise it; it had never spoken up before.

"There's someone here to see you," the nurse said.

The little hairs on my body bristled. Who could it be?

"There's always a concern," she said, "that an assailant will come here after an assault. Tell me now. Did someone do this to you? Like, were you attacked, or was this consensual, or…"

"Nobody did this to me," I said.

Something smacked against the glass of the hospital room door. The door was curtained, so I couldn't see what it was, but it wasn't too aggressive. Softer than a knock. It happened again, then a third time, and a fourth.

The nurse didn't seem to notice. Her gaze didn't flicker to the door, she didn't blink, she didn't turn. Not until the door opened, and the curtain ruffled from the breeze, and something flapped into the room with soft whooshes that rose to the ceiling.

"Nurse Rosalie?" a voice said from behind the curtain.

"There's someone here to see Miss Anna."

Who is it? I wanted to ask, but I was too focused on the swath of red that streaked along the ceiling, across the room, coming to rest on the top of the IV pole beside my fouled hospital bed.

"Erinyes," I breathed.

It was her. Mom's cardinal. She was bright, red, and beautiful—a stunning bird full of feathers, life, and sparkling brilliance.

And she had no head.

The curtained shimmied, slowly moving to the side to reveal another nurse, and behind her, my guest, whose lips and hands were trembling, and eyes wet.

"Oh, Anna."

I'd know her anywhere. Hair black like a lake. Raven feathers all shine and darkness.

"Liza?"

Everyone froze, including Liza and I, until I lunged forward off the couch and fell into her arms, burying my face into her long, sleek, black lake of a mane.

I held on for dear life.

Chapter Nine

"It's been so long," Liza said.

I watched Erinyes's shoulders move, her body twist as if she was preening. Or at least she thought she was. It would be a hard task with no head and no beak with which to preen.

"It sure has," I said.

It was hard to know what to say. Two decades had passed since we'd left Eden's Edge. Liza had escaped after being brutalized, and I hadn't known if she'd lived or died. I'd figured she'd died, but I'd refused to allow that possibility to be true. I, instead, imagined her as a stunning adult, with hair long and draped in the dirt like a bridal train, a gathering of children around her with eyes as dark and mystical as hers. She was a doctor, and astronaut, and played the violin in some eclectic quartet on Vancouver Island.

Seeing her now, the impossible seated next to me, I knew none of my dreaming had been truth, other than her being alive. But she looked amazing. Better than she should have after being to hell and back as a child.

"I thought you were dead," I said.

"And I thought you were a witch," Liza said.

This stalled me.

But I am, I started to say, but that wasn't quite right. I'm not only a witch. My mother was, so a part of me was, but…

"I don't know what I am," I said.

"You are magic," she said.

I thought of our last encounter and realized she had watched me change. She was a witness to my transformation from girl into beast—a murdering, horrid thing.

"I'm a monster," I said.

"We are all monsters," she said. "Bobby Pickton was a monster. The worst kind."

His death had felt euphoric in my hands.

"Let's not talk about that now," she said. With a trembling hand, she tucked a sprig of her black, shiny hair behind her ear.

"How did you find me?" I asked.

"I've been coming to the Crown," she said. "For several months now. I've been wanting…"

She folded her hands in her lap. Her nails were artificial, a beautiful navy-blue manicure, but it didn't hide that she picked at her cuticles until they were bloody. I had a keen sense for details and had already noted the tiny scars on her lip from chewing on it, those damaged cuticles, the way she held her knees together so tight as if sealing a fortress around her genitals.

"I'm glad you're here," I said. "And if you can't be here for long, if you have to go because it's too hard, that's okay, too."

Fat tears were rolling down her cheeks when she looked at me. "I missed you, Witch," she said, and tears trickled into her smiling mouth when she spoke.

"I missed you, Black Lake."

We embraced again and didn't let go. We sat there,

entwined, until the curtains flittered and Nurse Rosalie came into the room.

"Thought you said you had no one?" Rosalie said. She was smiling as much as we were.

"That's what you said at Eden's Edge when you first came," Liza said. "But you already had us, right from the moment we met you in that library."

Us.

The word was a knife in my neck. I swallowed hard, trying to rid myself of the pain of the blade.

Laz and Mary. They didn't fare as well as you and I, Dearest Black Lake.

"I have someone," I said to Nurse Rosalie. "Now."

"Long lost friends," Liza said and held my hand in hers.

"I'm glad," Nurse Rosalie said. "Anna here is in a bad way, and I don't mean the damage to her netherbits."

Liza looked at me then at my lap. "They told me you were brought here," she said, her voice edged in rising panic. "Did someone… Are you hurt?"

I was going to speak, to defend Gus, but Nurse Rosalie kept on going. "She doesn't eat well and hasn't been sleeping. This woman needs some self-care and some time off."

"I have bills to pay," I said. "And I don't get tips for sitting at home eating broccoli."

"Were you attacked?" Liza asked. "At the pub? Because some woman named Sheila said—"

"Sheila needs to mind hers," I said. "Yes, I had some troubles. Obviously, I was face down in the kitchen, but no. No one attacked me."

Nurse Rosalie gave Liza a look that wasn't reciprocated. Liza had seen things. She'd seen me, and she knew about impossible things.

"I think you should let us do the rape kit," Rosalie said.

"No," I said.

It was Rosalie, and she was asking nicely, and she meant

well so my voice stayed its own—single tone, quiet, non-confrontational. Regardless, that nagging voice—a language and tone not my own—clawed at the top of my diaphragm, scrambling to burst from my throat.

"You sure?" Liza asked.

"How would I explain this?" I said, motioning to my crotch.

Liza didn't know what I was referencing, but she didn't push. There was no room in a normal imagination to piece together what had happened.

"Do what's best for you," Rosalie said. "But can I at least have a peek? Clean you up a bit, make sure there's no real damage?"

I nodded. It was probably a good idea. The last thing I wanted was rabies, or an infection, or internal bleeding from Gus messing around inside me.

"Good, good," Rosalie said.

"No rape kit," I said.

"No rape kit," she said, making a cross over her heart.

I trusted her.

"I'll get everything ready," she said, "and we can take care of it across the hall in the exam room. Better lighting, all the equipment."

I nodded.

"And don't worry about those smelly coppers," Rosalie whispered. "I'll have 'em kicked to the waiting room before you cross the hall."

She touched my hand tenderly before picking up her chart, and gave Liza a wink as she left the room.

"How did you find me here?" I asked.

"Sheila." Liza shrugged.

Of course.

"I didn't see you at the pub, and you're usually working on Saturday nights. I…was worried you had gone. I finally got the courage to ask, and she said that you'd been violently attacked. They rushed you off to the hospital. She said that you just about died and still might."

By this time, only a mere few hours later, the story had probably grown fangs and bullets and…

…Four penises…

…And I could imagine Sheila re-enacting the whole ordeal with arms flapping and eyes wet.

"How long have you been around?" I asked. "Watching me?"

Liza looked at her hands. "You make it sound creepy."

"It's not."

Liza hesitated, didn't look up at me, but said, "Just a couple of… Well, maybe six weeks or so. I found your name in the system, came to the neighbourhood. I wasn't far, anyways."

"Where were you?"

Where did you go, after?

"I… Some couple picked me up on the side of the road. Brought me into Vancouver. Lots of cops and questions, but I was as forthcoming as you seem to be."

Now she made eye contact with me, and I melted. I was here, with wounds, pain, and aggressive police officers lurking like grotesques at the exit, and the warmth of friendship tingled my bones. Something I hadn't felt since my life before.

"I don't like cops," I said.

"Did the cops pick you up? From Eden?"

I nodded.

They had. The night that everyone had died, either by Allison's hand or by mine.

"How long did you stay?" she asked.

I have no idea. I was there while Eden burned around me, while feathers and flesh turned to ash. Then there were lights—red, blue, a disco in the trees—and I was gone. In the back of a car, in the hospital, in a home with other children I didn't know, and adults who pitied me, and a dwelling that was a mere Band-Aid across an arterial gash.

"You found me in the foster records," I said.

She nodded. "I found your name. First name, anyways. Noted the timeframe, months after, and found you. Anna Eden. Clever."

It was clever. Eden's Edge was death and rebirth. The end of what I thought I knew about myself and the beginning of the nothingness that my life became. I didn't know who I was. And I had no interest in learning. I wanted to be a regular kid, with a dead mom and dad, who lived in foster care, ate, slept, got hit, and fucked like the rest of them. I wanted to be a regular teenage runaway who stuck needles in her arms, sucked cocks for money, and slept in Stanley Park where the least amount of piss and vomit was. So, in short, yes. I was a product of my transformation. Of the events of Eden's Edge.

"It's legal, too," I said. "They let me have Eden as my last name. I figured they would have given me anything just to be done with me.

"Was it in the news?" she asked. "Eden, I mean. I was in the hospital. They interviewed me, and detectives kept coming to me. They knew I'd been out there, but I refused to say anything."

"Why?"

"Because…you were there. And I didn't know what happened after I left, and I didn't want you to get in any trouble."

The bones of a serial killer and a cult leader lay smouldering in the woods, and she worried that I would get in trouble.

"It was big news," I said. "I didn't admit to anything, and they didn't finger me. Bobby was there, and Allison, and the remains of…"

Everyone they'd taken, tortured, and slaughtered.

"They investigated, and Bobby was all over the news.

Allison got off scot-free. They blamed everything on him."

Which was fine. She got hers. And I knew, deep in my blood, that she continues to receive her karma in hell.

"What did you…" Liza asked.

"I razed it to the ground," I said.

We were quiet then, sitting on the plastic couch in my hospital room. I supposed we were both thinking about our lives, our brief lives in Eden's Edge, and the black void of time that hung like a haze between then and now.

"I've basically been waiting to die," I said.

Liza teared up. "Me too."

Erinyes ruffled her plumage, and a single feather twirled down and stuck to my IV bag. The crimson barb on the bag of clear fluid seemed like veins of garnets beneath the hospital lighting. Wet blood topped the stump where Erinyes's neck had once been, but she didn't seem to mind. Her chest rose and fell. I wondered if she was singing to us.

"Things were calm," I said. "Quiet. Almost normal, for two decades, then…"

The black of the private bathroom caught my eye, threatening me with the shadows it contained. The more I stared at it, the more I saw eyes there, watching me, and teeth ready to bite. The shapes didn't make sense: the toilet looked like a goblin, the sink the blade of a murderer. As I focused, and the lights of the hospital room dimmed around my vision, the shapes moved, swaying, chittering in the dark.

Friend was on her haunches on the toilet tank, rocking side-to-side, my soiled clothes in her mouth. She was sucking the blood out, the slurping noises amplified in the small space.

"Everything's back," I said.

"What's everything?" Lisa asked, her voice timid and scared.

"The ghosts," I said.

"Old Man Merle?"

"No. Not the ghosts, I suppose, but Gus. And New Friend. But she's just Friend now. Neither of us are very new anymore."

Liza was patient. She obviously had no clue what I was yammering on about, but she listened. "I want to hear all about it," she said. "All about you."

"And I want to hear all about you," I said.

"Are you really okay?" she asked. "Physically, I mean."

Friend had my entire gown sucked down her throat. The fabric bulged through her onion-skin flesh.

"Physically, yes," I said.

"Then let's blow this joint. Get you somewhere more comfortable."

"Can we just go home?" I asked. "To my place?"

I had no clothes. And no desire to see any more monsters, or humans, or human monsters.

"Absolutely," she said. "I'll get us an Uber."

"I hope you don't mind," I said, waving a hand over my fresh hospital gown. "But I came in wearing less than this. Is it…okay?"

Liza shrugged out of her long coat and wrapped in around my shoulders. "I wouldn't care if you walked out of here in your forest suit, Witch. All skin and folds and spots."

I laugh-cried, and Liza laughed and cried too. She left the room first, and I followed, and we snuck down the stairwell like schoolgirls escaping a college dorm, at a college we'd never seen, in a life we'd never been lucky enough to have.

Chapter Ten

I told Liza everything. Starting with Gus's initial birth at Eden's Edge, to Erinyes and her decapitation alongside Mom's death, to Miss Mojo and her bugs. I had trouble telling her about what I did—transforming and slaughtering Bobby Pickton, and Allison in her irregular suit and gruesome smile. I also didn't tell her about the throne of bones Old Man Merle had made for me, or that I ate the hearts of my mom and dad.

I also told her about Friend, the old version and the new. It felt like a betrayal of sorts. Friend was mine—my secret, a part of me. As I was spilling all my guts to Liza, Friend hung in the corner of my kitchen ceiling, her long hair dangling down to the counter as I spoke. Liza's return felt odd, even though Friend had been back for only a few days longer. I wasn't used to friends and didn't quite know how to navigate the two of them.

I told Liza about foster care, and my income source, and drugs, and all the things I needed to remain above the grass instead of below. Yet it always felt like I was one day closer to death.

"Are you sober?" she asked as I poured us another glass of wine.

"No," I said. "But I'm in control."

I always was.

Even an eight ball and a two-four of whiskey barely made a dent in my coherence. It was moments like those, when I should have been blackout stumbling and raving beneath an underpass, that I realized I was, in fact, not like other girls. That I wasn't a girl. That I was something else entirely.

Half-bred, tainted, rotten bitch!

I tamped down the voice in my head with a gulp of my Merlot.

Someone like me couldn't get high or drunk. But it did take the edge off, if only just a little.

"Mom was a witch," I told her. "And I spent my childhood with her. Learning, observing."

"And your dad?" Liza asked.

"A demon."

Liza listened but didn't react.

"I killed him. That's why we had to come to Eden's Edge."

I know I hadn't told my new friends anything when I first met them at Eden's Edge. But the end of our time together was a blur. I didn't remember what they knew.

She. Not they.

They knew nothing. Not anymore.

THEY DRINK RIVERS OF SHIT IN HELL.

That voice in my head again; unwelcome and sultry. It was a violation, and my whole body shuddered in repulsion.

"So… it's all back?" Liza asked.

"Not all of it," I said. "I'm seeing things. New things. Some of it I'm seeing again, but differently."

"You're not ill, you know," she said.

I was going to deny that, to say that yes, my symptoms

were the very definition of a mental illness, but I knew better. Though I didn't know what I was, I knew I was in my right mind.

"I just want to be normal," I said.

"But you're not," she said.

She hadn't meant to be cruel, but it stung. But it also didn't. I didn't feel wrong. I just felt like me.

"I'm not ill. What bothers me is not knowing what I am."

Same old story.

Liza glanced out the window, at the bustle of the city, the looming figures of glass and steel, cold and heartless. "You've lost touch with nature," she said. "Remember how much you loved the woods? And your garden?"

I hadn't seen more than a patch of grass or a single weed in years.

"People are dying," I said.

Liza's head snapped in my direction. "Now?" she asked, looking around my apartment.

"Not here. People I don't know," I clarified, "but there were two. A guy in the dumpster behind the pub, then a lady at the grocery store."

"Vancouver is volatile," Liza said. "Fentanyl addict in the dumpster? I heard them mention it at the pub. It didn't even make the papers."

"Yeah. Probably. But…"

Liza watched me, studied my face.

Was she afraid?

"What are you thinking?" she asked.

"I'm thinking that in all the years I lived in the street, and now here, and working in a grungy pub, and the death …"

She was watching me so closely my skin started to crawl. I looked down. Embers coated my body, singing the hair on my arms. The smell of burning flesh was pungent. I took a long, slow sip of wine and a full breath from my glass to drown the stench. A commotion erupted in the corner;

Erinyes had taken wing and was flying into my window, smashing against it and splattering it with blood.

Suppose she can't knock her head off this time.

Liza didn't seem to notice, so I pretended not to as well.

"Those deaths are too close in time and proximity," I said. "With Friend back, it all seems like too much of a coincidence."

Friend crawled off the counter and skittered across the carpet in front of us until she reached Erinyes and the window. She grasped the bird. Erinyes went into a frenzy, squirming and writhing. If she'd had a head, I imagined she'd be screaming bloody murder.

"It's probably a coincidence," Liza said. "Unless there's something you're not telling me."

Friend put her fingers on the lever and opened the window ever so silently, just enough to allow Gus to slide inside. Once he was in, and the window shut once again, Friend released Erinyes, who gave her a stern beating with her wings before coming to rest on the windowsill beside Gus.

"There's more," I said. "A drawing in blood, at the grocery store where the second body was."

"What did it say?" Liza asked.

"It wasn't words. It was hearts."

I told her about the diner. About the fingerpainting New Friend did for me the night we met.

"Oh," Liza said.

"Yeah," I said. "Oh."

Erinyes couldn't preen Gus, but he cleaned her, combing her feathers with his claws and licking away dirt. Once that was finished, they curled up together in a ball of feather and fur, no eyes and heads visible.

"So, what are you thinking?" she asked.

"I don't know."

IT WAS YOU WHO KILLED THOSE PEOPLE, YOU HALF-BREED, TAINTED…

I froze.

The voice in the head, accusing me at the volume of a gong in my skull.

"I'm not a murderer," I said.

Liza startled. "I…I didn't say you were."

"Sorry," I said. "Not talking to you."

Liza searched the corners and shadows. "Is she here?" she asked. "Friend?"

Friend was in the kitchen. Her chest was pressed into the countertop, her spine curved into a 'C', the soles of her feet framing her face beside her gaunt cheeks.

"Yes," I said. "On the counter."

Liza squinted, searching for some variation in the void, but I supposed all she could see were countertops and cupboards.

"Does she scare you?" Liza asked.

"She's only me," I said, brushing it off. "Somehow. A part of me I don't understand."

And I scare me.

Liza touched my hand. "You must be exhausted," she said.

"I am." I was. Completely, all of me, physically, mentally, and spiritually drained.

"Me too," Liza said.

"Let's rest," I said. I stood from the couch and led her to the bedroom.

I thought of lending her a pair of pajamas, but she stripped out of her jeans and sweater as soon as we entered the bedroom. She was unfazed by this exposure—she folded her clothes and laid them across the chair, wearing nothing but pastel panties and a white tank top. The soft colours made her skin glow a dark shade of gold and her hair a glimmering raven's wing. I had always found her stunning. Right from the moment I met her.

I was too shy to undress. I took my jammies to the

bathroom, where I changed behind a closed door. My mom would have been sad. Shame was not in her vocabulary, and she'd be disappointed it was now in mine.

"You are beautiful, you are powerful, you are strong," she'd tell me, but I was anything but. Most days, I wished I was an armadillo that could curl up in the protection of a shell, roll to work and back without anyone being able to poke me through my armour.

When I came out of the bathroom, Liza was standing beside the bed with a sheepish expression as if aware of her state of undress.

"I'm sorry, I just, should I…" She looked out the bedroom door at the couch beyond.

"Crawl in," I said as I did just that.

She crawled in beside me. We lay on our backs, studying the spackled stars on the ceiling. I listened to her soft breathing. Her scent of vanilla and lavender was so subtle beside me. Soon my eyelids grew heavy, and her breathing slowed. I rolled onto my side, facing the wall. She was asleep when she turned into me, wrapping her arm around me and pulling me close. Her breasts pressed against my back, the air filling her body when she inhaled, and her warm breath on my neck. I focused on that—on every feeling, smell, and sound of her as I faded into a peaceful slumber.

Chapter Eleven

I t could have been a good night. The beginning of a wonderful turn of luck, a new life. Liza, my friend, a friend beside me. I wasn't alone. She knew the real me and hadn't run screaming. We were bound by a horrific past and deep magic that entwined us in a way no one else could understand.

I was sound asleep, peaceful for the first time in a long time, when a colossal bang from the apartment above shook the ceiling.

We both shot straight up in bed.

"What was that?" she asked, looking at me as if I knew what was transpiring with my upstairs neighbour.

"No idea," I whispered, as if what was above might come below.

Another bang, this one louder, was forceful enough to jiggle the chains on the ceiling fan.

My feet hit the floor first. As I went to the door, Liza fell behind to pull on her clothes. I hesitated before opening my apartment door. I put my ear to the wood, trying to hear if there was anyone in the hallway, but only an ocean of oak filled my ear.

"Someone out there?" Liza asked.

A gleam from behind me caught my eye. She'd grabbed the largest knife from the block in the kitchen.

Smart.

"*As are you,*" Mom's voice reminded me.

BUT YOU DON'T NEED TO BE SMART, NOW DO YOU? BEASSSSTTTTT.

"Stop," I said to that unwanted voice in my head.

"Stop what?" Liza asked.

WHO NEEDS SMARTS WHEN YOU CAN TEAR A HUMAN IN TWO?

"No," I yelled.

Liza didn't have any more questions.

Another bang from above was quieter, and it didn't stop at one.

Bang bang bang.

Like raps from a fist, the banging continued, rhythmic, persistent. Almost like someone was knocking on the floor.

"Do you know the people above you?" Liza asked.

I shook my head. I didn't know anyone in my building. I kept my head down, my business to myself, and left everyone else to theirs. I pressed my ear to the door again.

"We should maybe call the cops," Liza said. "I know you don't like them, but—"

I opened the door, and my stomach lurched. Friend was there, hanging upside down on the outside of the doorframe. She touched her nose to mine, and her teeth chittered together as her black serpent of a tongue tried to form words. Her body contorted, and her bones creaked and cracked as she used her hands and feet to crawl down the door frame until her soles were firmly planted on the hallway carpet. Then she rotated her head, so it was no longer upside down and took my hand in hers.

I let Friend lead me into the hallway. Liza followed as we went past the elevator and to the stairwell, pushed our way through, and ascended to the next floor.

The lights in the fifth-floor hallway were flickering. Liza moved closer to me, pressing into my back as Friend led me to the door I sought.

"This is the one?" Liza whispered. "Right above you?"

Friend nodded.

I knocked.

"Anna, what are you doing?" Liza whisper-shouted at me.

Like an echo from my knuckles against the wood, the knocking continued on the other side of the door, slow and rhythmic.

I knocked again.

"Hello?" I called out. "I'm your neighbour from downstairs. We heard a bang. Are you okay in there?"

Bang. Bang. Bang.

I knocked again. Then a fourth time. I was about to leave, call the cops like Liza suggested, but Friend held tight to my hand. She tugged my arm, spread my fingers, and placed my hand on the door handle.

"Anna, what are you—"

The door opened.

"No," Liza said. "We can't… This is breaking and entering."

"It was unlocked," I said.

I looked at Friend. I expected her to go into the apartment first and take the brunt of whatever was banging on the floor, but she didn't. She gave me a firm hug, scaled the wall like a spider, and scampered off across the ceiling until she was back in the stairwell.

"Thanks," I said.

"What?" Liza asked.

I walked into the apartment. Liza followed, and once we were four steps in, standing at the edge of the kitchen, the door clicked shut behind us.

"Anna, I don't like this."

Neither did I, but we weren't at ground zero yet. The banging wasn't coming from the kitchen or the living room but from the bedroom, behind yet another closed door.

Bang. Bang. Bang.

I flipped the kitchen light switch. The fluorescent bulb jittered to life with a hiss, illuminating a grotesque palate of filth. A sink full of dishes covered in algae and mold, raw chicken on the counter that had turned grey-green and was crawling with maggots. The white tile floor was streaked with brown and red and stank of shit and copper. My feet squished into the swampy carpet that was saturated in fuck knows what fluids as I crept towards the bedroom.

Liza was pleading with me, but I couldn't decipher the words above the noise coming from the other room. My ears were filled with the screams and mewls of anguish, the tearing of flesh, the chipping of teeth against pavement. Bones snapped, bowels gurgled and splashed to the floor, and animals screamed as if being slaughtered. And all that noise was coming from the bedroom. But I went in, anyway.

"Hello?" I said as I walked in.

No one answered me. They couldn't. They were already dead.

The occupant of the apartment was in his bedroom but not tucked all neat and cozy into bed. Bed bugs would have been preferable to the fate he'd suffered.

He was strung up to the ceiling by his ankles. His body had been sliced nearly in half; there was a deep incision that started at his rectum, followed the seam of his testicles, dissected his cock in two, and continued in a chasm that splayed him open from groin to throat. He'd been exsanguinated, his insides pooling on the carpet below him in a meaty, muddy mess.

Liza was screaming now, and her voice was hollow,

echoing in the empty sockets where this man's eyes had once been.

"Kaz," I said. "Kaz Hill. We need to call Kaz."

I had an alibi. This wasn't me. I reached into my pajama bottoms for my phone, and when I brought it out to tap in my passcode, I couldn't. My hands were wet. My fingertips smeared blood over the screen.

Friend was sitting criss-cross-applesauce below the hanging body, poking his forehead with her finger, causing the body to thump into the wall.

Bang. Bang. Bang.

Her hand was covered in blood, too. The hand that had held my hand. My hand, that was now covered in blood.

I wiped the phone on my pants, entered in the passcode, and pulled up Kaz's number. I hit dial, and as the phone rang, Liza turned on the bedside lamp.

"Anna."

More artwork on the wall, above this man's headboard. Two large hearts framing a smaller one, all squeezed together, blood trickling down in streams from the bottom. But there was more to this one. The blood trails looked like roots, and at the end of their path, they were smeared into the wall with globs of wet brown and pink matter that I knew, I just knew, belonged, at one time, to the inside of that man.

But it really was pretty, the roots on that heart tree.

"Hello?" Kaz said.

"Hi," I said.

"Who is this?"

"Anna."

"Oh, Anna, hi… It's late… Are you…"

Through the phone came the squeak of a bed. I wondered if a wife or girlfriend was beside him, if he had little kids with tight ringlets sleeping soundly in the room next to his. I was standing in carnage, and I imagined it seeping through my phone screen, out through his, and drowning his pretty life and pretty little family with gore and death.

"I'm up," he said. "What's going on? Where are you?"

I prattled off my address and hung up.

"Is someone coming?" Liza asked.

She was trembling and quiet with fear.

She should be scared.

I didn't answer. I left the apartment above mine, the home of a man I didn't know, a man who was no longer, and I went to the stairwell. As I walked down the concrete steps, I made sure I didn't slip; it was no easy task considering the steps were covered in footprints of blood, shit, and vomit. I was leaving a trail of death, but there was already a trail coming from the fourth floor, going on the fifth. And two sets going down.

YOU WERE UP THERE.

"I wasn't," I said to the stairwell and the unwelcome voice.

YOU WENT UP, RAVAGED THAT BLOKE, CAME BACK DOWN TO YOUR POOR, SCARED LITTLE PLAYTHING.

I peered over the stairwell at the spiraling tunnel to the floors below. I was on the fourth-floor landing, looking down. I had been here many times, on my floor, at this spot, but it was so very different now. It went down, down, down, past the first floor and at least eight more besides, and didn't stop there. There was bubbling blood waiting at the bottom, filled with smoking hair and singed flesh. Dead animals swam in that hell water, screaming as the liquid melted them, then their bones, and still they continued to bellow. I screamed with them, matching their pitch and adding some rage.

STOP.

FUCK OFF.

DIE AND BE DEAD, YOU CURSED CUNTS.

But the screaming continued.

I went through the fourth-floor door to my apartment and crawled into my bathtub. I rolled into an armadillo ball. Friend curled around me, latching her multi-jointed limbs together to secure herself as my armour. I closed my eyes and wished it all away, far away, deep within the dirt and eons below the black of the sea.

Chapter Twelve

"Do you need another minute?" Kaz asked.

I needed much more than that. I needed a full lifetime to process what was happening. Actually, I'd rather use that time to avoid thinking about this. I could cram it in the back of my throat, swallow it, and tamp it into my intensities where it could fester and rot, and I could forever forget about it.

"I require more than a minute," I said.

Kaz stood beside my couch where I sat, head in my hands, trying to pretend I was the only one in my building. It was a hard thing to do, what with all the foot stomps and ruckus from above. Doors clicked open and shut—looky loos poking out their busybody noses to see what drama had occurred in the night.

Is it still night?

My blinds were open, just a pinch, but enough to see the red and blue lights flashing against the opposing building.

"What time is it?" I asked.

"Early," Kaz said.

"Or late, I suppose."

He nodded.

"Please sit," I said.

He was making me nervous, hovering above me like I was carrion ready for consumption.

"I …" He hesitated but relented.

I was occupying the middle cushion, so it was hard for him to sit as far away from me as he probably would've liked, but he damn well tried. When he lowered himself on the side cushion, the arms of my old couch creaked against his weight as he pushed against it, trying to put every little millimeter of distance he could between us.

"I know it looks bad," I said.

"Anna," he said. "I really don't get the sense you'd be capable of…that."

I caught the snap of Liza's head as she watched me from the kitchen.

She knows I'm a monster.

YOU ARE A MONSTER, YOU HALF-BREED, TAINTE—

"I could be," I said. "You don't know me."

"I know *people*," he countered.

I am not people.

"I had nothing to do with these deaths," I said, even though I didn't quite believe it.

"But there is a connection, yes?"

I nodded.

"One at your work, at the grocery store where you shop, and right above where you sleep."

"I know it looks bad," I repeated.

"Can you think of anyone who might want to hurt you?" he asked. "Who might be mad at you?"

No, I killed everyone who had beef with me.

"I don't know many people," I said.

Kaz glanced at Liza.

"She just got here," I said before he asked.

"From where?" he asked.

Eden's Edge. And I sure as hell wasn't going to tell him that. The last thing I wanted was anyone looking into that fire, into that area, into me. My records were sealed. I was a specter in the real world—a girl with no past.

And no future.

"I live on the Northside," Liza said. "Anna and I were childhood friends. We had a fight a long time ago, as girls do, but I stumbled across her at the Crown and Anchor. It's been nice to reunite."

Holes like Swiss cheese. All it would take was a single question directed at Sheila, and she would spill at the details—Liza asking about me, sitting at the bar alone night after night. Kaz would smell a lie and look deeper, all the way to the center of the province where Eden was hidden in the woods, waiting like a dirty secret to out me and ruin my life all over again.

"Whereabouts on the Northside?" he asked.

"Here," she said, grabbing a pad of paper and a pen out of her bag. "I'll write down the address."

While they were busy with the details, I took a minute to acknowledge Friend, who was crouched in the corner behind my drapes. There was no need for her to do that; no one could see her but me, not even Liza. Friend was listless, shifting from foot to foot, gnawing on a mouthful of her hair. But the poor woman seemed tormented. Guilty, maybe? Whatever she was, she was in distress. Every so often she'd open her mouth wide and scream, spraying black spittle over the backside of my curtains, then bite her arm violently and spit the chunks of necrotic flesh onto my carpet. I wanted to comfort her, but my apartment was full of people who were already debating whether I was crazy or dangerous or both.

"I'm tired," I said.

"I know," Kaz and Liza replied in unison.

He flipped his notebook closed. "I have what I need for now."

He sat beside me and spoke softly as if I were a child with no hair, mouth, and eyes to see the horror but was scared nonetheless. "It's okay, Anna," he said. "We have a full investigation ahead of us. We're taking into consideration that you may be a target rather than a perp."

I didn't like the sounds of target any more than I did perp.

He reached out to pat my arm but then must have thought better of it. His hand hovered over my shoulder before he pulled it back and looped his thumb in his belt.

"*Todâ raba*," I said.

Though those words came from my body, it wasn't me who spoke. It wasn't a language I knew, and it wasn't my voice. It was my mom's voice. It was different from the vitriol I spewed at Officer Empusa. This voice was a song.

Kaz stared at me, let a half-smile tug at one side of this mouth; he didn't know whether to laugh or be concerned. I didn't know, either, but given the circumstances, I'd lean towards concern.

Liza shuffled him to the door. I watched as his feet crossed the threshold into the hallway, the door closed behind him, and Liza's bare feet approached the couch.

"What was that?" she asked. "That language? What did you say?"

I shrugged.

"You don't know?" she asked.

I shook my head.

"But how…" Her brow softened, but her shoulders were high and tight. "Has that happened before?" she asked. "Speaking…"

"In tongues?" I forced a smirk. "Only one other time that I know of."

"Eden?"

"Yesterday," I said. "In the hospital, to one of the

detectives questioning me. I had no control of the voice, just like with Kaz, but the voices were different.: the one that spoke to Empusa and the one that spoke to Kaz."

"I…" Liza bit her lower lip. This was a lot. I was a lot.

"I know you're not okay," she said, "so I'm not going to ask if you are. But I want you to know I'm here. You wanna talk? Scream? Break some glasses? Throw kittens off the balcony?"

I kinda did. All of the above.

"It wasn't me," I said. "Those dead people."

"But you think it might be," she said.

She had known me for such a short time but knew me so well.

"Yeah," I said. "I wonder."

"You were in bed," she said. "With me. I didn't feel you get up."

"You were sound asleep."

"I never sleep that well. Not since Eden."

Me neither. But I didn't have to be asleep to be removed from reality.

"There was blood on your hands," she said, both a statement and a question.

"Friend," I said. "She had blood on her hands, and she led me to that apartment."

"I could see the blood," Liza said.

"Yeah."

"But I can't see her."

"… Yeah.…" Valid point.

"The cops think you touched the body."

"I did," I lied. "When I noticed the blood on my hands, and on Friend's, I purposefully put a palm on the body. Easy to explain why it was there than to try to clean every bit of it off.

"I think they bought your explanation."

"I hope so."

Didn't matter what they bought, or sold, or assumed. The evidence would eventually paint a picture, like that artist who painted on the wall of the bedroom, the grocery store, wherever else they were leaving a message.

But no one knows about it but me.

"That image," I said. "The triple heart. New Friend drew that on the window of the diner."

Liza nodded. "But there was more to it, yes?" she said. "This one? There were…"

"Roots," I said. "Veins."

"So, someone is adding to it."

"Adding to something no one could possibly know about?" I asked.

Liza suggested, "Have you considered it might not be… some*one*?"

"What do you mean?" I asked.

I think I knew what she meant. Did a person murder that junky, the man upstairs, and the woman at the grocery store? Or was it something not quite human?

Friend was still in the corner, munching on her hair and fiddling with the blobs of flesh on the carpet. I slid off the couch onto my knees and went to her. She winced like I was going to hit her.

"I know you didn't do this," I said.

She cocked her head, eyes wide and leaking black fluid.

"It's okay," I said. "I'm not upset."

She opened her mouth and keened, then fell into my arms. I embraced her, avoiding the sharp angles of her four elbows and four knees as she crawled into my lap. It was like a Great Dane sitting in the lap of a toddler, this ten-foot-tall arachnid woman curled in my embrace.

Liza watched. She couldn't see Friend, but she didn't ask. I assumed she knew why my body was bent beneath an unseen weight, my arms wrapped around an invisible bulk.

"You see things," she said. "That aren't there, but really,

they are."

That was true. It's not that they weren't there, it was just…

"I straddle a veil of sorts. I experience more. Sometimes I see the world through witch's eyes," I said, gesturing to the creature she couldn't see on top of me, "but I also see other things. Darker things."

A thick, profane demon, the crackle of the fires of damnation.

"Part of me is a darker thing," I said.

"Right. So, if your mother were here to help you, or Miss Mojo, we might find some answers. But what if that's not what this is? What if this is…"

"My Dad's side," I said.

"Darker things," she said.

"Demons."

He's come for me. My dad. His hell is picking up speed in my veins, outpacing my mom's witch blood.

"Hear me out," Liza said. "Maybe we need not consult a witch, but someone who is more of an expert, in say, matters of the devil and his cronies?"

"An exorcist?"

Her head shook, but not with any conviction. "No, maybe not that, exactly. But the church."

As a staunch atheist, the thought of consulting a business full of liars, charlatans, and abusers didn't thrill me. "I don't believe," I said.

"Then what was your dad?" Liza asked.

"A demon," I said.

"Which would argue the existence of hell," she said.

"Not necessarily," I said.

She huffed and sat on the couch. She was trying so hard. And I was so difficult in every way. I was the beginning, middle, and end of all my problems.

"You're right," I said. "It can't hurt. There may be

education in the church."

One witch wasn't the expert on all witch kind, and the religious weren't the wisdom holders of all things unholy. That didn't mean I couldn't find nuggets of truth from either.

"There's a Catholic church by my place," Liza said.

"Good fucking Christ," I sighed. "The Catholics?"

She shrugged. "Go big or go home."

I wanted to say no, to stand up and tell her to leave. I'd go back to the bar and live out my days blissfully unaware. But I knew better. The demons, the darkness, the murders weren't going to disappear. They'd find me—follow me until I was on the wrong side of the grass.

Besides, only so many people could be ritualistically murdered in my orbit before they toss me behind bars to rot, and then some.

"It's a date," I said.

What does someone wear to the house of God, if that someone was the embodiment of all things unholy?

Chapter Thirteen

Cathedral of Our Mother of the Blessed Rosary was a stunning piece of architecture. I had passed by it many times, walking to and from work, when I was out shopping, or when I was aimlessly skulking about. I had never paid it much mind, though. When I did happen to notice a church, I'd glance elsewhere and think of dirt, flowers, and red feathers. All churches big and small, rich and poor, reminded me of The Beast back in Eden. They all had mouths ready to chew, throats with which to swallow, and bellies ready to melt me down to nothing but waste.

I'd be lying if I said I wasn't intimidated as I stood in front of the grand wooden doors. The church's spire towered overtop of us, and I waited for it to snap off, spear through the air, and pierce my heart.

OR YOUR BELLY, WHICH HOLDS BOTH HEART OF MOTHER AND FATHER.

"You are not welcome here," I said to Unwelcome Voice.

Liza said nothing. She knew I wasn't speaking to her.

Whoever owned that voice didn't belong here; its tone and

cadence were unholy. Some dirty little demon infecting my mind with its syphilitic cock, fucking the folds of my brain, and driving me to madness.

I AM WELCOME WHEREVER YOUR FEET TOUCH GROUND. WHEREVER YOUR FLESH AND ORGANS OCCUPY SPACE.

"No," I said. "Not if I don't welcome you."

It laughed, its voice cruddy with plague and infection. I AM NOT UNWELCOME, it said. I AM TREBOR.

My breath hitched and stomach clenched. *Did the demon within me just name himself?*

"Isn't that a dangerous thing?" I asked. "Don't I rid you by speaking your name?"

Another laugh, and this time its breath coated my nostrils with soot and pus.

"Trebor," I whispered, half-expecting, mostly hoping, that uttering his name would cause him to vanish, or to shrivel like a cold cock, up into his own being, never to be heard from again. It didn't do any of that, but it did shut him up. Not entirely, but I could deal with the sound of his wet breath rather than his rancid words.

"Who is Trebor?" Liza asked.

Friend wondered, too. She lingered beside me, glaring, but not at any creature that stood near. No foulness perched atop my shoulders that she could claw, bite, and fend off while I went inside. She was glaring right at me, her wrath and hunger palpable in the small space between us.

Part of me, for the first time, tingled in fear of Friend.

"Let's go inside," Liza said. "If that's okay."

It wasn't. Nothing was okay, but it was never going to be, no matter how long I delayed, waiting for everything to right itself.

The door creaked open with a groan that hollered our arrival to the inner cavern. And once it slammed shut, barring us in with the silence, I realized we might be the only ones inside.

"Is it open?" I asked of the church.

"Churches are always open," Liza said.

"But what about vandals? Theft?" I asked.

"It's not unattended, I'm sure," Liza said.

It seemed like it was, though. As we walked into the chapel, our footsteps called back at us from the cathedral ceilings, a metronome of our approach. There was no one in the pews, at the pulpit, nor near the confessionals or intention candles. But there were flames flickering, and soft hymns echoed through the chamber like an orchestra hidden within the moldings on the ornate ceiling.

"It's beautiful," Liza said as the stained glass spilled tinted sunshine over her face.

"Ugly," I said of the glass that was unnatural, forced in designs and shapes to please the eye.

The flowers littering the stage were plastic, with no scent or movement of life that ever was or would be. There was nothing alive in this place. Even the wood that made up the walls, seating, and ornamentation was repurposed, stolen from its home, placed in this building where it was ignored and forgotten. A backdrop, a white-noise of visual ambience that no one cared a single good god damn about.

My mother's lullabies sang in my ears, and out of Friend's throat as we made our way up the aisle. It was a mournful keening, a blessing for the death of the wood in that building.

We arrived at the pulpit. I stared into the eyes of the artificial Christ that hung there, gazing pleadingly out at his would-be masses, begging with his eyes to be taken down from his death, his eternal pain, his reminder that he was a mere flesh, bone, and blood pawn, constructed just like the forgotten wood of these buildings of manufactured, razzle-dazzle faith.

"I'll see if I can find someone," Liza said. "Are you okay here on your own?"

I nodded, even though I wasn't okay. She disappeared down one of the halls, an arm leading from the belly of this beast, just like the tentacles of The Beast back in Eden's Edge.

I hated churches. Everything about them, everything that happened in and because of them, and anyone associated with the madness.

I took a seat on the front pew, trying to understand the beauty that Liza saw. It did warm my heart…

HEARTS

…though that she found beauty at all after being struck with such ugliness as a child. I was amazed she'd not only survived, but had grown, lived, and maintained a bit of that blue spark in her coal-black eyes.

In front of me, Jesus's hair was growing. Long tendrils of his greasy mane pooled over his face and his chest, hiding the gash in his ribs.

"Hey," I stage-whispered as I startled out of my pew. "What are you doing?"

Friend was attached to the dome of the ceiling, her hair draped over the crucified fiction. When she let go, I nearly screamed. She landed on the Jesus with a hard thud that shook the whole building. Her talons dug into Christ's shoulders, piercing the paint and the plaster with a crack that sounded like breaking bones.

I stepped onto the pulpit and approached the Christ, swinging my arms like I was shooing away a crow. "Get," I said as plaster crumbled onto the carpet.

Friend lifted off, taking wingless flight and latching onto the dome of the ceiling. Pieces of Christ rained down, flecks of paint and plaster that littered the entire pulpit and the first few rows of pews.

Another cracking rang through the church, and more plaster fluttered to the floor. But Friend was on the dome, watching and still. My gaze lowered, coming to rest on the damaged Christ. Puffs of dried plaster farted out from his crotch, and hairline fractures spread up like diseased veins from beneath his loincloth. =

Christ's thighs and shins split. The plaster fell away completely, revealing bulging black legs beneath. The loincloth was next, torn away by two serpent cocks that rose and coiled up the ribs of Jesus, snapping away plaster with their fangs until all the plaster was shed, exposing the entire the body of The Unwelcome—the demon who'd stalked me in the alley behind the pub.

"What do you want?" I asked.

It couldn't speak through the mask of Christ's face—painted eyes rolled up to the ceiling, mouth drooped. The Unwelcome made no attempt to remove it.

"My dad," I said. "Did he send you?"

Growl and drool leaked from below the Christ mask. The snake-cocks hissed and slithered up and down The Unwelcome's body, striking at his flesh.

"You aren't welcome here," I said.

YOU ARE. SO I AM.

"Trebor?" I said.

The Unwelcome flinched at his name.

"You are the one in my head," I said.

Trebor grunted an acknowledgement.

"Murder follows you," I told him. "As you follow me."

YOU. IT FOLLOWS YOU ALONE.

The snake-cocks grabbed the mask on either side and pulled it from Trebor's face. Tacky blood and globs of fat stuck to the inside of the mask, peeling away like hot cheese from flesh, leaving lumpy dough and tomato sauce behind. Trebor flexed his muscles and tore his wrists from the crucifix one at time then kicked his hooved feet until he was free. I took a step back as he took a step forward, then I retreated no more.

You are strong, Mom said in my head, her voice a

harmony of all the gentle, good voices.

I stood my ground. "You do not scare me," I said.

When he moved forward once more, I was revealed a liar as my body trembled, and my feet told me to run. But I didn't listen. I flexed my muscles, balled my hands into fists, and glared with all the heat and hate in my body.

Something shifted within me. A stirring, an awakening. Friend dropped from the ceiling and landed behind me. She pressed her chest against my back, entering me, like she had so long ago. And she emerged, her long talons sprouting from my fingertips, her height stretching my torso, my arms, my legs until I was nose-to-snout with Trebor. I swiped a talon across his throat to end him as I'd ended Allison, but it was ineffective. The bone of my talon bounced off his solid throat with a ting like a dinner bell.

That's when the cocks got me.

The snake-cocks slammed into the sides of my head, penetrating my ears, while the main cock swelled, becoming erect. Before I could react, the snake-cocks, that were brain-deep into my skull, slammed my head down, my mouth open in shock, onto Trebor's phallus.

He didn't want to fuck me. Though his dick was hard, he wasn't rubbing on my tongue or moving into me seductively. He was trying to split me in two. The wispy tongues of the snake cocks were tickling my grey matter while his main cocked lifted me off the ground, spinning me upside down, pushing deeper and deeper, becoming a solid bulge at the top of my stomach. Once he was swollen to the peak of erection, he came, and came, and came, bloating my stomach and swelling my intestines. I couldn't handle it. Semen leaked out of my ass, my vagina, and forced the snake-cocks out of my ears with geysers of demon sperm. I couldn't see through the hazy yellowing gobs dripping from my eyes. I was choking, both on the thick meat jammed down my throat and the snot-semen filling my sinuses and gushing out of my nose.

A pain in my chest alleviated all the horror.

My eyes cleared, licked clean by a swipe of Friend's tongue. My chest was on fire. I looked down where her arm was plunged first-elbow deep into sternum, creating a drain for the semen flooding my body. It poured out in a frothy waterfall over the pulpit, down the stairs, and beneath the pews until the entire floor had a sheen and my body was empty and deflated.

Trebor was gone. Left in the place where he'd stood was Christ's mask, floating in a semen puddle in front of the podium on the pulpit. The sunlight filtering through the stained-glass windows strengthened, burning bright and drying up the fluids. The puddles rose to fog that dissipated and dried until the chapel was clean once more.

"You okay?"

Liza was standing at the edge of the pulpit, staring at me as I huffed and puffed on my hands and knees.

"What's that from?" she asked, pointing at the Christ mask on the floor.

There was no plaster on the carpet, no signs of destruction. Only me and the mask.

"I'm not sure," I said.

She knew I was lying. I could tell by the way she tilted her head and squinted her eyes, by the weak smile on her lips. But she didn't push any further.

"Did you find anyone?" I asked as I wobbled to my feet.

I couldn't act like there wasn't something wrong. My head throbbed, and my throat was raw. My body ached from being filled then emptied. I staggered and braced myself on the podium as the world swayed.

"What the hell happened to you?" she asked.

I didn't answer. I couldn't open my mouth for fear that she would smell the vile semen still coating my tongue. I swallowed hard, hoping to smother the gag rising to choke me.

Liza wrapped an arm around me and led me down the stairs to the aisle. I guessed she hadn't found anyone because she was leading me towards the door.

"There's a library," she said. "Down in the basement. I found a clerk in the back who said we could go there and check it out. But we should come back another time."

I shook my head. We were here, and I wanted this over with. We headed to the basement, Liza supporting my weight, stopping only for me to grab four paper cone cups of water from the cooler to wash the foulness from my mouth.

Chapter Fourteen

I knew everything about libraries but nothing about churches. And church libraries were just as foreign to me—tomes of threats, fear, and flights of fancy. The history was interesting, but most of that seeped with warped truths. It was a small library, of course; it contained only catholic and catholic-adjacent materials. The myriad spines of cloth, leather, paper, and wood were daunting at best, hopeless at worst. What were we looking for? Books on demons? Unexplained phenomenon? Mental illness?

But I wasn't too worried. I knew we'd have help.

As Liza tackled the exorcism section and I scanned the shelves of apocalypse literature, Friend creaked through the aisles, sniffing and licking the dust off book spines. She'd helped me once before, in the house that was a library in Eden's Edge. She'd found the book that I needed. I hoped she'd do the same now.

"There are endless volumes on exorcism," Liza called. "But I'm not sure that's quite what we're after."

"No," I said.

Trebor growled from between the rows, hiding in the shadows, his voice a rasping panting that followed me every step I took.

"Go away," I said to Trebor.

Liza winced.

"Not you," I clarified.

Friend was hunched in the doorway, braiding her arms and legs together.

"Finished looking?" I asked her.

"No, I… Oh," Lisa said. "You aren't talking to me."

She was going to get fed up with my random dialogue.

"It's not one-sided," I explained.

"I know.

"I'm not just jabbering into the void," I said.

"I scream into that from time to time," she said.

Her smile lit the whole library. I couldn't help but smile, too. I gave her the biggest, tightest hug.

"What's this for?" she asked.

"I'm so happy you're here. That you found me."

"Me too," she said. "It's what I was waiting for."

Neither of us moved. I held her, and she me, and the heat from her body made mine tingle. I became acutely aware of her curves, her smell, the whole-hearted way she hugged me front-on. I wondered if we would meld into one like Friend and I do, if we could live in each other's skin and be with each other for all of time.

"No, no. There'll be none of that."

Liza gasped, and we pulled apart. There was a little old lady at the doorway, hunched over a walker, glasses on the tip of her nose. She looked at us and clucked her tongue.

"The clerk said we could come here," Liza said. "We're just doing some research on a project, and—"

"Did he say you could come down here and canoodle?"

"We weren't—" Liza started to say.

"If we were canoodling, you'd know," I said in the voice

within me that wasn't quite mine. "There'd be tits out, pussies gaping, and we'd squirt geysers over these books."

A darkness swelled in me like Trebor's cocks. A rage, violation, a loss of control—the marionette strings piloted by my father's thick, calloused fingers.

Liza gawked at me, Friend crawled away from the old woman, and the crone swallowed a mucousy breath. The thump thump thump of the old crone's heart against ribs weakened by osteoporosis. The fetid stench of bowels filled the air as the gas of fear leaked from her decrepit body. The scratching of Friend's nails as she clawed at her teeth with anxiety.

"Excuse me?" the crone said.

I took a step towards her, and a voice came out of me, one that wasn't mine but lived in my belly. And on those words was the taste of semen, thick and salty, that bubbled on my tongue and in my nose as the voice leaked out in a bitonal growl.

"Have you tasted pussy?" the voice asked. "You just fold it open like a book and…"

My tongue flicked out, long, forked, and black, and I licked it between my fingers that I held in a 'V' in front of my face.

Friend rose to her feet, walked to me, and slapped me across the face, causing me to bite my tongue.

"Anna." Liza caught me when I stumbled backwards, thrust off-balance by the force of Friend's blow.

"I… Oh my god, I'm so sorry, I don't know what came over me," I said.

"You should go," the crone said. "Get out! Now."

"Yes," I said. "We'll go, straight away."

"And don't return," the crone said when I shuffled by her, dragging Liza behind me.

As we charged up the stairs, I looked back to check if Friend was following. She wasn't. She wasn't anywhere, but

I knew she'd pop back up at some point and startle the shit out of me. What I did find, though, was equally startling.

The old woman was there, hunched over that walker, pushed down by the weight of the demon riding her back. Its legs were folded and tucked into the back of her blouse, causing that hump that old ladies get. I wondered if other old ladies had riders, too.

What did you do?

Having a rider meant you had a sourness in you. A certain badness, a taint of evil. I hadn't seen riders since the bout with the serial killers and rapists of Eden's Edge. I didn't wish to begin seeing them again.

"Again," I said. "We're very sorry."

The crone's tongue clacked, and the rider cackled as we ascended the stairs and burst out of the church and into blinding daylight.

Chapter Fifteen

"What the fuck?" Liza said as soon as we were on the street in front of the church. "What's gotten into you?"

"My dad, I suppose."

Parts of him were coming out. I wished the part of me that was Mom would wrap its arms around his throat and squeeze until he was no more.

"Do you ever feel your mom?" Liza asked.

"Bits and pieces," I said, thinking of Erinyes back in my apartment. "Not much anymore. Not since leaving Eden's Edge."

"I have another idea," Liza said.

She pulled out her phone and started poking at the screen. I scanned the rooftops, watching pigeons warbling at each other and pecking at bugs and stone. In the mass of grey was a swath of red. Erinyes was strutting through the pigeons, dodging their pecks and swaggers.

"Up for a walk?" Liza asked.

"Yeah."

Walks cleared my head. Walks were outside, and I longed for the outside: plants, trees, any fresh air I could find.

I also, at that moment, wanted to be away from that rooftop where the pigeons had swarmed Erinyes and were tearing her feathers off, leaving her bald. The plucked feathers twirled down from high up above when the blood sprayed as they started pecking and ripping at her meat.

Was I losing Mom completely? Would Dad soon take over?

"Let's go," I said.

"This way," Liza said, pointing in the opposite direction.

I looked straight ahead and walked through the piles of feathers on the ground—what was left of Erinyes and her headless body.

Liza and I didn't speak the whole way to our destination. My head was loud with the sounds of distant, muffled mewling, and my mouth and nostrils were still salty with the tang of semen. It felt like I had downed pots of coffee and an eight ball. My body was chaos, my mind a riot. Everything was too fast, too loud, and too hard, and—

Liza took my hand. The noise and clutter decrescendoed as I focused on the soft skin on her palm, her pulse, her heat. She held tight, pulling us together. Her breathing was low and purposeful. I slowed mine to match hers and we fell in stride together.

"Here," Liza said as she looked at her phone screen.

I lost track of how long we'd been walking or how far we'd come. I was happy to see the church spire was far behind us, obscured by buildings that no longer loomed overhead. We'd strolled out of the sea of concrete and glass and into the outskirts of residential bungalows and strip malls. Liza had stopped in front of one of these little shopping centers. This one was dilapidated and nearly empty—four vacant spots, a nail salon, and a dry cleaner. There were two businesses that were open but didn't have any signage. A bakery, judging by the window full of rye breads and donuts, and a trinket shop.

"Which one?" I asked.

"Gotta be this one," Liza said, pointing at the thrift shop.

When we entered, the little bell dinged, announcing our arrival like a danger. And I felt like an invading troop standing on this foreign land. The shop was filled from ceiling to floor with knick-knacks, papers, mirrors, cloth, and crystals. There was a spicy aroma of incense that greeted us, and the air was hazy with the smoke of the burn.

The chaos in my mind reignited. The incense started to smell like pine on fire, and the glow of Eden's Edge on fire flickered on the ceiling, thrown by flames below that weren't there.

"Can I help you?"

This time it was a little old man. He was hunched over like the crone, but he didn't have a rider. Not that I could see. Yet.

"I googled," Liza said, "and your place was on the list."

"What did you google, dear?" he asked.

"I, um… Well, it's a little silly, but…"

"Witchcraft? New age? Something along those lines?" he suggested.

Liza nodded. Then shrugged.

"Demonology," I said.

His smile straightened from a large curve to a tight line. He gave us the once over before coming around the counter.

"Yes, we dabble in that too," he said as he pointed to the shop name carved into the wooden counter front. "Fantastical Flights of Fancy,"

"Fuck. Fuck. Fuck," I said in Trebor's tone, alliterating the excess of 'F's' in his moniker.

Liza squeezed my hand.

"Sorry," I whispered.

YOU AREN'T.

"I am," I argued with Trebor.

YOU ARE LOSING CONTROL.

"I am not," I spat in my bitonal garble. "I won't."

The shop owner was watching me carefully, as was Liza.

"Schizophrenia?" he asked Liza.

"I know that's what it seems like," she admitted.

"But you think not," he said.

"I'm sorry," I said as tears welled in my eyes.

"Ah. Well, be that as I may, the name's Olliver," he said as he dipped into a curtsy.

"Anna," I said, tapping my chest.

"Liza," she said, doing the same.

"All right then, Anna and Liza. Let's have a look-see."

Oliver spun on his weathered loafers and went to the back of the store where he pulled a curtain aside to move even deeper, out of the store proper and into a cozy lair of all things dark and decrepit.

"Mostly for show," he said as we passed into the dim room. "The Satanists love burgundy walls, black furniture, and candlelight."

"Any truth to it?" Liza asked. "Hell and demons and all that?"

"Who knows?" he said. "But many spend a great deal of time contemplating it."

I moved along the perimeter of the room, taking in all the trinkets, the bundles of hair and bones, the taxidermied animals, the jars of bloody body parts. There were books, too, but it was far too dark to make out what was written on their spines except for gold embossed symbols or publisher's stamps.

"Searching for anything in particular?" Olliver asked.

"We're doing a research project," Liza said, "on demons."

"Wide topic," he chuckled. "There are endless demons. What faith interests you?"

Liza looked at me.

I shrugged.

"Well, let's start with the basics," he said. "People seem fascinated by the seven deadly sins. That's where all the fun is, I suppose." He coughed out a laugh and plucked a laminated chart from a bookshelf. "Here," he said. "We sell a lot of these."

I took the sheet from him and read it to myself.

Lucifer: pride

Mammon: greed

Asmodeus: lust

Leviathan: envy

Beelzebub: gluttony

Satan: wrath

Belphegor: sloth

Baal: fear

"Agrippa's classifications are more in-depth, separating specific demons into numerical classes. Starts with Lucifer himself, the one prince of rebellion, angels, and darkness. Nine classes in all. One for elements: earth, wind, water, fire. One for direction: north, south, east, west. Then there's the biblical class that refers to the nine princes ruling over the nine orders of devils: Beelzebub, Belial, Mammon, all those fellows."

Olliver fetched a dusty hardcover off the shelf and thrust it in my direction. It was massive, with browned pages and a curled cover.

"You talk of elements," I said. "And directions. How do witches factor into demonology?

He didn't answer straight away. He studied me, his lips in neither a smile nor a frown. "Why, witches are demons," he said. "They are of the devil."

"What about paganism?" Liza asked.

"Listen," he said. "Anything in opposition to or violation of the so-called God's law was considered demonic. It all falls under the same umbrella. But you ladies seem the sensible type. I don't think I need to tell you that it's not so simple."

It was too much. The heavy book in my hands, the myriad tomes sitting on the shelves. The answer was a grain of sand in all the beaches of all the oceans. We didn't have a hope in hell of finding what we were looking for, especially because we didn't know what that was.

"My mom was a witch," I said.

Liza audibly gasped.

"Anna, no—"

"And my dad was a demon," I continued. "I killed him, and Mom and I ran. I have powers. I see things, and I… I'm not normal, and now there are things happening, bad things, and—"

Olliver held up his hand. "Hold on, my dear," he said.

I didn't hold on. "I don't know what I am," I said. "Or what I'm capable of. I was close with my mom, and I wanted to be like her. I thought I was like her until I realized I was, in part, like Dad."

"Yes, but you are forgetting one very important thing," Olliver said.

I sniffled. A few tears had escaped, and I didn't realize it until they ran into my mouth. Liza held my hand.

"You forgot the part of you that's you," he said.

I cocked my head.

"You are comprised of both mother and father, yes?"

I didn't answer.

"Semen and egg, then infant. But that was as a little baby. Their flesh, blood, and bone is what keeps you together. And their traits—you undoubtedly have some of those, too. But you grew up in your world. Not theirs. Your growth is not only your blood but how the world around you shapes your brain. You took the roots of your parents and grew into your own tree. Windy? You grew crooked. Seeded in the dark? You grew small and wide, requiring little light. Grew in the desert? Dry as fuck with thick bark and leaves of leather."

"Yes, yes," Liza said. "Nature versus nurture."

"Precisely, but not quite," he said. "It's not an issue of versus. It's a collaboration. And also, we're not dealing in normal plasma, tissue, and neural connectivity. We have smashed together demon and witch, volatile and magical. The consequences are…*fascinating.*"

Did he mean to eat me, this deflated little man? His mouth was wet with the sheen of saliva as he opened it to lick his lips. This delighted him, the anomaly that was me.

"Okay, but how does this help me?" I asked.

"It seems you have come to me, young lady, with an existential situation, correct?"

"Precisely, but not exactly," I said, parroting his contradiction. "People are dying."

It was Olliver's turn to cock his head. "You haven't told me precisely what's been going on," he said.

"I'm surprised she told you what she did," Liza said.

I was, too. But then again, I did tend to blurt. Always had.

"Murders," I said.

Liza flinched again.

"Oh my," Olliver said.

"Yeah," I agreed. "Three so far, all in proximity to me. The cops, well, this one cop is keeping an eye on me."

"Did you commit these murders?" he asked.

"Not that I know of," I said, unsure.

"Okay. Did you interfere in any way?" he asked.

"The first died in my arms," I said. "I found him after he'd gotten hurt."

"Ah, so. You did not do that murder," he said with a comforting nod.

"It's unlikely," I admitted.

"Unlikely? Are you prone to losing time?" he asked.

No, I wasn't. I saw impossible things, but I never had blank spaces. Or hadn't… "Not that I've noticed."

"Anything else to lead you to the conclusion that demons are involved?" he asked.

"Things from my past," I said. "I see things."

"Hallucinations?"

"I guess so. But parts of them are really there. Markings on walls, blood on my hands, big black devils with four cocks," I admitted.

"Golly," Olliver said.

Golly indeed. The taste of that semen curdling up like heartburn.

"You said markings on walls?" he asked.

"A design," I explained. "I saw it first as a child, drawn by…one of those things I see."

"And it's come back to haunt you," he said.

"Yeah."

He worked his jaw. It almost looked like he was sucking on his teeth, moving them around his mouth to help him think. He turned to the bookshelf and talked to the spines, passing very close to Friend, who was also examining the reading material.

"My loves," he said. "Will you give me some time to think on this? I need this information to simmer in my brain. Like soup. Gotta draw out information like flavour."

"Of course," I said, anxious to leave now that I'd spilled my guts.

This old and withered man had every right and reason to call the cops on me. And maybe he should. Maybe no one was safe around me. I squeezed Liza's hand, and a scene flashed before my eyes. It was her in place of the man in the apartment above mine. Her hanging by her ankles, insides on the outside, her dark hair pooled in her blood and entrails on the white tile floor. Her hair and Friend's hair were tangled together, and Friend made a slurping sound as she ingested Liza's lower intestines like spaghetti.

"Anna," Liza said.

I blinked. She was in front of me, hands on my shoulders, right side up and not hanging.

"Did you lose time?" Olliver asked.

"No," I said. "Just saw something."

"Huh," he said. "And I'm guessing drugs and alcohol don't work on a lady such as yourself."

I shook my head.

Liza shot a glare at Olliver. "Who are you?" she asked. "How do you know so much about…so much?"

"Well," he said. "Perhaps I'm a demon myself." Then he laughed, a multi-tonal bray that rattled the jars on the shelves.

"May I have a pen and paper, please?" I asked.

He obliged, and I jotted down my phone number and address.

"If you think of anything," I said.

"Oh, I hope to," he said. "And Anna?"

"Yes?"

"Go easy on yourself. You are Anna. You are smart. And you are strong."

My blood froze in my veins. It was not my mother's voice that came out of him, but it might as well have been. Liza took my hand again and led me out of Fantastical Flights of Fancy with our haul of literature and zero answers.

Chapter Sixteen

I had to go back to work. Despite that fact that there'd been dead bodies all around me, that I'd had a traumatic birth experience, or that the cops suspected…something, if I missed a shift I'd lose the tips, or worse, get fired. So in I went. Liza protested, of course, but she needed to go home, change, and shower. I didn't need a babysitter, anyway, though she was much more comfortable leaving me at a crowded pub rather than below the very fresh crime scene at my apartment.

It would've been a quiet night at the Crown and Anchor—weeknights tended to be—but the Canucks were playing the Oilers, which brought fans out in droves. I didn't mind hockey nights. Patrons were loud but focused on the ice on the screens, which meant less small talk, and the thrill of the game led them to eat and drink more, which meant bigger bills and tips. So I poured liquor as Sheila ran food and helped myself to a few shots along the way. Not that it made much of a difference, but I pretended the Iceberg on my tongue would chill me out, if only as a placebo.

During the second period break, a chap with a man bun—peeking out beneath his toque–sidled up to the bar. From the way he sauntered, he thought he was pretty smooth, and the way he leaned forward meant he wanted more than just another Kilkenny.

"Hiya there," he said. "Patrick."

"Nope," I said. "Name's Anna, not Patrick."

He laughed, showing all his teeth, and I thought of a Loup Garou stalking the woods of Stanley Park, waiting to howl at the moon, fuck stray dogs, and devour human flesh.

"Witty," he said. "Anna, I'm pleased to make your acquaintance."

"For everyone?" I asked. "Or just you."

"Huh?" he said.

"The next round," I said. "You buying for your whole table or just for yourself?"

Another laugh. More teeth. "Fuck no," he said. "Those losers are on their own."

I'd already poured another Kilkenny, which I slid in front of him after adding it to his tab.

"Whoa, you really know how to please a man," he said.

I pert near gagged. Came extra close when he made a point of maintaining eye contact with me as he licked the foam on the top of his pint. I was going to redirect this by asking him if he wanted anything to eat, but then I thought better of it. For sure he did, and it wasn't on the menu.

"Lemme know if you need anything else," I said.

He did want something else, but I didn't stick around to hear. I was already in the kitchen, the door swinging behind me, hiding around the corner so Patrick couldn't see me through the pass.

"Creeper?" Robbie asked.

"Yep."

"Want me to jizz on his wings?"

"He didn't order any yet. But yes. When he does, go to

town."

Robbie cheered and jumped up and down, those fucking crocs slapping on the floor when he landed.

I sang through a full Tragically Hip song before returning to the bar. The third period was about to start, so Patrick had taken a seat at his table with his buddies. I noted that there wasn't a single vagina in their group and was thankful I'd only had to deal with one of them so far.

The whistle blew. Everyone directed their attention at the game, giving me a chance to take a piss and grab a drink and a snack.

"Shelia," I said, beckoning her to the bar. "If any of that lot orders food, let Robbie know it's the wing table. No matter what they order."

She scrunched her brow but agreed, then flitted off to flirt-up her tippers. I passed through the kitchen, shut myself in the employee bathroom, and sat on the toilet, not planning on moving for at least ten minutes. But I got no such peace. As soon as the flesh on my thighs hit the cold seat, there was a knock from the back door.

"Can you get the door?" Robbie bellowed. "I got thirty fucking things here on the go."

And from the manic squeaking of his Crocs that had to be true.

I hiked my pants back up, washed my hands, and entered the bathroom just in time for whoever it was to knock again.

"Can I help you?" I said as I pushed the metal bar, opening the back door to the alley.

There was no one there.

I took a step outside to peer down the alley. "Hello?" I said, and my voice echoed back to me. Except it wasn't just my voice. It was a cacophony of voices, low and high, dry and wet. I looked up and saw Gus, Erinyes, and Friend watching my every move.

"Hello."

This one came from behind me and was most definitely a real voice. I startled and let go of the door, which shut with a click.

"Hi Patrick," I said as I eyed the door.

I pulled the handle. Locked again.

We're doing this again…

"Sorry, I don't mean to be a weirdo," he said, "but I—"

"Why are you back here, Patrick? Did you knock on this door?"

"I did."

"Don't." I had no patience for this.

"I just wanted to talk to you," he said. "Alone."

Now my hackles were really up. All I could think about was the body in the dumpster, the corpse at the grocery store, and the hanging man at my apartment. Who was this guy, this Patrick? I'd have to look up Patrick the Patron Saint of Hornery or whatever, but part of me did wonder…

"What do you need to talk to me about?" I asked. "I pour drinks inside."

A smirk curled his lips. "I want a drink," he said, taking a step closer. "But not from inside the pub."

He leaned in. So did I. I didn't give him another chance, and I didn't politely tell him no, or make excuses why I needed to leave. I kicked him square in the balls.

He dropped to his knees, huffing and grunting. I started off towards the front of the building. I only traveled a couple strides before he grabbed my ankle.

"You fuck," I said, but it was too late.

He whipped his legs around, swiping my feet from under me, and when my head hit the concrete, I saw stars. I let them swirl. I pretended to be at Eden's Edge, laying in the cemetery with New Friend one side, Old Man Merle on the other, Gus chirping away in the trees …

Gus was chirping. Screaming, in fact.

I came to my senses to find that Patrick already had my

pants off and his knees between my ankles.

All I could think was: *Huh, now there really will be a rape after all.*

With one hand, he squeezed my breast, and with the other, he pulled his cock out of his jeans. It was nothing impressive, but I was surprised how erect he was after taking a blow to the bollocks.

"Fuck you," I grumbled.

He was too horned up to notice that it wasn't just my voice, but a duet of tones swirled together in a harmonic slurry.

"Oh, you will," he said, "And you might even like it, if you give yourself a chance."

I tried to knee him again, but he let go of my wrist to catch my leg. I took that opportunity to claw four gouges across his face before he gave me an uppercut, snapping my jaw shut and rattling my brain in my skull.

Again, stars. My eyes fluttered shut and I still saw them, explosive white bursts on a black background. He panted as he ripped my panties off. The goo beneath his foreskin stank like cheese as he rubbed the head of his dick over my labia, trying to lube me up and find the opening.

Something changed within me. Awakened.

My eyes snapped open. I punched a hole in his chest with my taloned hand, splintering his ribs and piercing his heart. It took him by such surprise that he was still hard when I sliced off his dick with my other talon and dangled it in front of his face.

"Fucked, you say?"

With a heave of my hips and a twist, he was on his stomach eating a mouthful of alley water and filth. I didn't bother to shimmy his jeans off like he had mine. I simply shredded away the fabric with a few swipes of my talons. Then, with my knees between his, I spread his legs and stuffed his cock up his ass. The now-useless tube of spongy meat needed some help getting into such a tight spot, though, so I thrust it in with my talons, slicing his lower half to ribbons in the process.

"You like that, baby?" the other voice said with my mouth.

"Holy fucking shit," another voice screeched.

Patrick was dead. He wasn't speaking, and it wasn't Trebor, and there should be no one here. But there was. The backdoor to the restaurant was ajar, and there was Robbie Cum Crocs, mouth agape, lips white, and eyes wide in shock.

"What the—" he stammered.

He didn't recognise me. I didn't know what I looked like, but I was certain it wasn't like me. But how would I explain…

I could explain none of this. Not to myself, to Robbie, to Liza, and the cops.

Robbie hit the ground with a bone-crushing thud when I tackled him. I shredded his clothes, too, including those noisy motherfucking Crocs.

I had a hard time inserting them, but anything will go where you want it with enough force. I shoved one shoe down his throat, dislocating his jaw and ripping his esophagus in the process. The other shoe went up his ass, which I had to pull and push and prolapse a bit before it tore a straight tunnel through to meet its mate. Once the Crocs were reunited, and Robbie was very much dead, I rocked back on my haunches and surveyed the scene.

Blood. Meat. Hair. Clothes. It was a right mess. Thank fuck it was dark, late, and that everyone was watching hockey for…

I tried to look down at my watch to see how much time I had left but my rippled, scaled arm had burst through my leather strap. I could be discovered at any moment. Sheila'd need food and alcohol, and the period must be over.

Go back inside. Clean yourself up. Pretend nothing happened.

But a great many things had happened. All over that alleyway. I couldn't leave it like this.

Friend was there, tugging at Patrick's ankles.

"What?" I asked. "What do we do?"

She was trembling as bad as I was and frantically hauling Patrick towards the dumpster.

"They'll find him there," I said.

But she didn't intend to toss him in. She dragged him behind the dumpster, then hopped on the edge and pointed at Robbie.

I didn't argue. It took little effort to hoist Robbie over my shoulders, leap over the dumpster, and pile him on top of Patrick.

"Now what?" I asked.

Friend crawled down beside the body heap, poked at the skin, then placed a finger on her black, sore-encrusted tongue.

"You have got to be kidding me."

But she wasn't. She took the first bite.

"Should we pray first?" I laughed and cried as she ripped a glob of meat from Patrick's thigh and swallowed it whole. I watched his flesh travel down her near translucent skin, between her breastbone, and into her stomach where it roiled and digested.

"Fuck."

I started with Robbie's hands, biting off a finger with my powerful jaw and grinding the skin and bone until I could swallow it. I went finger by finger, and once I was done with his hands, I looked over to find Friend had devoured all but Patrick's feet. She rolled her hands in a hurry-up motion.

She's right. I better hurry unless I want more trouble.

I worked his limbs down my gullet like a snake and gorged myself on the fattier parts. I didn't even pause to breathe. I ate everything but the clothes, including those fucking crocs. Friend and I tossed the two sets of clothes and footwear into the dumpster.

"They'll find that," I said.

And I didn't care. I was exhausted and horrified. And absolutely stuffed.

Friend had a plan. She leaned into the dumpster, her long stringy hair pooling in the leavings of pub food, and struck her nail against the metal inside. A single spark ignited the whole mess, and within seconds, a raging fire was licking up the building on either side of the alley.

RUN, she mouthed.

"*RUN,*" Trebor screamed in my mind.

So, I ran. I started off towards the mouth of the alley, but Friend grabbed me and pointed up before she scaled the wall like a spider.

Can I?

Turns out I could. My talons retracted, I jumped at the wall, and the pads of my fingers and soles of my feet stuck tight. I squelched them off the brick, leaving a trail of slime as I crawled up that building until I reached the top.

I wasn't even out of breath. And it was a fourteen-story building.

Friend and I sat side-by-side on that roof, our legs dangling over the edge, watching the glow of the flames below. Erinyes landed on her shoulder, and Gus scurried up on mine as the firetrucks arrived, assaulting the entire neighbourhood with their lights and noise.

My mind and heart had calmed, and my flesh and bones constricted back to normal. My body was my own once again—pale flesh, slender, short nails chewed raw. I was naked, and I cursed my fair complexion, wondering if I was a beacon in the night sky. But we were far up. And I didn't care.

I leaned against Friend's breast and dozed. Whatever transformation had taken place had drained me, both physically and emotionally. I cried as I slipped in and out of consciousness. I wasn't worried about falling. She held me tight, rubbed my back, and warbled a soft melody into my ears. It sounded like a quartet of cellos, dark, warm, and soothing. I wondered if we could just stay there forever, let the world go on without us. We could die here; our bones could degrade to dust and blow off on the west wind until we reached the ocean. We could rest on the beach with the sounds of the Pacific splashing against the earth until the end of all time.

Chapter Seventeen

I did not stay on that rooftop forever. I waited until just before dawn and climbed down the zig-zagging fire escape on the opposite side of the building. I snagged a blanket from a nearby homeless encampment, wrapped myself up, and ran home, taking all the back and darkened routes. The Crown and Anchor was abuzz with activity when I left, but the farther away I got, the quieter it became. By the time I reached my apartment, I could barely hear any activity at all.

I gave myself a pat on the back for having the foresight to climb up my own fire escape and in through my balcony. My building was still crawling with cops who were investigating the hanging man upstairs. They were also patrolling the premises and interviewing the neighbours. It seemed like so many moons ago we'd found that guy upstairs, but it had been less than forty-eight hours. So much had happened…

…AND WILL CONTINUE TO HAPPEN, Trebor sneered in my mind.

"Oh, fuck off, will you?" I shouted as I slid my door open,

dropping the stiff and filthy blanket on the patio before going inside.

I lingered in my shower until the water ran cold. I used soap at the beginning, when there was still steam, then again in the ice-cold chill. I still didn't feel clean. Once I was out of the shower, I stood naked in the bedroom in front of the mirror and examined myself.

It was me. The same me I'd always known. As a little girl, I examined my vulva, my body, and all my nooks and crannies, as little girls do. But I didn't know then that there might be something wrong with me. That I wasn't a normal little girl. Now, examining myself as an adult, I felt wrong. I was an abomination.

I took my time, standing close to the mirror with all the lights on and walked my fingers over my body, searching for deformities, abnormalities, anything at all. I traced along the curves of my flesh, seeking odd muscles or bones that weren't quite right or didn't quite belong. But everything was where it should have been, as far as I knew.

I tossed on a T-shirt and pajama bottoms and plunked myself down on the couch. I had brought a bottle of wine with me in hopes that somehow it would magically intoxicate me and soothe my nerves, but truth be told, I liked the taste anyway. That's another thing I'd like, when the bone dust from Friend and I came to rest on the ocean, would be a fine bottle of wine that could actually make me tipsy, the fresh fruit of the Okangonan sweetening my tongue.

EVERYTHING YOU WANT IS IMPOSSIBLE, Trebor said.

"Everything I am is impossible," I replied.

I flicked on the television to drown his voice, my voice, and the panic of solitude. I picked my favourite streaming service and chose a period drama with elegant gowns and British accents. While the main character prattled on about how Louis had been fawning over her which was simply *awful* because it was with George her heart truly belonged, my mind wandered to my body, to how foreign it was to me, and I imagined the monster I was becoming—a scale-covered, murderous beast.

"No," I said to myself.

I left the mistress and her friend on the screen to debate the trivialities of too many romantic options and went to snoop in my freezer for ice cream. I found an old Drumstick hidden in the back corner—probably freezer burnt, but good enough.

I had all the lights off in my apartment, so the flickering light from the yellow-washed show cast ominous shadows. It should have scared me, but it didn't. I was a shadow myself, waiting in corners, closets, and under beds, salivating over my next victim.

"It was me," I cried through my mouthful of ice cream.

It must be. All the dead people around me, my transformation, the vile creature that whispered sour evils in my mind.

Tchaikovsky's *Grande Valse Villageoise* was playing on the television, and all the characters were waltzing around the room, gowns swishing, feet tapping an echoing staccato that reached the vaulted ceilings of their very Baroque palace. It was all so divine. What wasn't divine was shoving a squirrel inside of myself. What wasn't exquisite was the stench of semen in my nose, or the human flesh gurgling in my belly.

I didn't want it anymore, this uniqueness. At one time, I thought it was magic, being a witch. I'd studied all the witches in history, and I'd read about root magic, possibilities, the beauty of the craft. Then Eden's Edge happened, and I realized there was filth in my veins. I was a…

HALF-BREED, TAINTED, ROTTEN BITCH.

"Stop," I screamed, but Trebor's chant continued in my head.

HALFBREEDTAINTEDHALFBREEDTAINTEDHAL FBREEDTAINTED

The characters on the television were swirling and twirling, dresses like plumage filling the screen, smiles wide, mouths open, laughing and kissing.

I danced, too, and I sang along to the Tchaikovsky music, trying to drown out the noise in my head.

"I know you…" I sang, and the television sang back at me, but it wasn't pretty, or in tune. I dared to stop mid-spin and look at the screen even though I knew I shouldn't, and I found the horror I had anticipated.

The characters on the screen were no longer dancing. Their layers of clothing—a myriad hooks, fascinators, buttons, and crinoline—were littering the floor as they fornicated violently, tearing and breaking each other with snaps, thrusts, and bites.

"*I know you…*" the central figure on the screen sang as he locked onto my eyes.

Familiar beings danced on the screen, amongst the humans. Trebor whirled Friend around in a pirouette as she struggled to get away, but he had one massive paw on the small of her back and the other, talons and all, around her throat. As she squirmed, black pitch poured from her mouth, rectum, and vagina. Her skin sloughed off like onion-skin bible pages, floating to the floor and coming to rest with the piles of clothing.

I tilted my head. She tilted hers. I bent my knees and dug my feet into the carpet. Her knees bent, and her reptilian feet flattened to the floor of the ballroom, the claws at the ends of her toes drilling through the wood and holding her in place. Trebor tried to spin her, and when she wouldn't budge, he tried to lower her into a dip. I saw it coming, so I stiffened my spine.

I fully expected my body to change, to become that horrible brutal thing from the alley, from Eden's Edge, but I didn't change. Friend did, though. She got bigger, wider, her bones swelling, her hair growing until it tangled around Trebor's hooves. He released her neck and moved his hands to her chest. He tried to push her away, but now it was her turn to hold on. Her arms lengthened and wrapped around his bulk, and though she was still but a willow tree compared to his girth, she was unbreakable. He thrashed and mewled as she wound her limbs around him like ropes.

The ballroom was filling with that black pitch pouring from her every orifice. I knew then what her plan was. I watched as glittered clothing floated in the black lake and all the lace, silks, and satins changed from red to brown to black. Soon the liquid lapped against Trebor's throat as he tried to swim, but Friend held him down. The water rose above his eyes, his horns, and soon the whole screen was black and rippling. Tchaikovsky was still playing, but it sounded like a quartet beneath the ocean playing its swan song. And there was screaming, so much as Trebor's breath choked out of him in bubbles filled with gasps until it quieted, and slowed, and…

The television exploded with a bang. Hot, black pitch surged over my apartment in a wave, carrying my furniture to the kitchen and me along with it. Everything was soaked and black, but I was more concerned with the bloated, blue bodies scattered over my carpet. It should've been the characters on the show—that's where these things came from, right? But it wasn't. It was my people, from my past and present, all naked and bulging with the gasses of death, blue from the airless bottom of the black lake.

Dad. Mom. Miss Mojo. Liza. Mary. Laz. Robbie. Sheila. Everyone.

I tried to scream, but black pitch came out of my mouth and nose. I sucked in a breath but fluid filled my mouth and lungs, and the pressure in my chest was excruciating. My ribs expanded like I might explode, then they cracked. I fell to my knees and clawed at my throat. I was determined to pierce a hole there so that air might pass, but the heel of my palm came to rest on my chest and what I felt there stopped me.

Thump. Thump thump. Thump.

My heart was beating, but it was irregular like an entire percussion section. The volume and tempo increased, but I was calm now. My breathing was free and steady, but my heart was an entire drum line banging inside my ribs.

Hearts.

More than one.

A knocking came. It wasn't my heart. Then it banged again, louder, closer.

Then a smash and splinters of wood rained into the black slick of my apartment.

"Anna."

Kaz was standing in my splintered doorframe, weapon drawn, several Mounties flanking him. He took a step towards me, then pinwheeled his arms. One of the other officers caught him before he fell.

"What the fuck?" he said.

The bodies were gone, but the black fluid wasn't. My apartment was slick with it.

"I…" I didn't know what to say.

He lowered his weapon and came to me. "Anna, what happened here?"

"I…" …Still didn't know what to say.

They were talking now, the flanking Mounties, and Kaz was at my side, guiding me to my feet.

"Come with me," he said to me.

"Have someone come get a look at this," he said to the Mounties, pointing at my floor, my furniture, my everything.

"Are you hurt?" he asked me.

I shook my head.

"Want us to get a bus anyway?" a Mountie asked Kaz.

"She needs to come with me," he said.

"Where are we going?" I asked.

"Why are you wet?" he asked.

"May I change?"

He hesitated.

"I'll go with her," Detective Empusa said.

I froze. She thudded into the room with that off-kilter gait of hers, bringing along the stench of manure and spoiled meat.

"What are you doing here?" I asked.

"We were called out," she said.

Kaz gave her a look.

"We've met before," Empusa said. "When she was in the hospital. The rape."

"I wasn't raped," I said through gritted teeth. The meat of my would-be rapist roiled in my belly.

"Whatever," Empusa said. "Go get changed."

I hated that she followed me. Her gaze was on me the entire time as I got naked, slipping out of my pajama bottoms and tank top to put on a hoodie and sweatpants. While my back was turned, she was making some sort of noise—a hissing from the pit of her throat.

"Pardon?" I said and found her staring at me with too-large, glowing red eyes that flickered with fire. A blink and that fire was extinguished, leaving normal eyes in their place.

"I didn't say anything," she said.

But there was something. I knew it. I'd heard the hiss, and I'd seen those eyes.

Empusa waited until I walked out of the bedroom first, then she followed, her feet making that weird, thump-clank-thump I'd noticed in the hospital. Once we were reunited with Kaz, he led me by the arm out the door. I looked back at Empusa, who was smiling at me. She was standing crooked; one of her legs appeared shorter than the other and her knees were bent at different heights in her pants. And her shoes were quite clearly two different sizes…

"Come on," Kaz prompted. "Let's hustle."

He was talking to me, but he was looking at her when he said it. She unsettled him, too.

Chapter Eighteen

"What's the rush?" I asked when we cruised down the backstreets in Kaz's car. It wasn't a police car, which I supposed was normal—he was a detective after all, not a beat cop. But he didn't have his siren on, and it seemed like he should by the speed we were going.

"I'm on your side, you know," he said.

That surprised me. I hadn't really thought about there being sides in the first place, but I did feel like I'd done something wrong. Criminal, even.

YOU MURDERED AND ATE TWO MEN, Trebor said. AND THAT DOESN'T COUNT ALL THE OTHER BODIES.

"Shut the fuck up," I said aloud.

Kaz's brow furrowed, and he touched the brake when he looked over at me.

"Not you," I said, staring at the passing scenery. My reflection showed my pale cheeks and untidy hair.

"Then who?" he asked. I caught his face as he glanced at me. I forced a shrug.

"The voice in my head," I said.

"So," he said, releasing and tightening his grip on the steering wheel, "you do hear voices," he said.

"Yeah," I confirmed. "But I'm not schizophrenic."

"What would you call it?" he asked.

I don't even know.

HALF-BREED, TAINTED, ROTTEN BITCH, Trebor offered.

"You know the Elizabethan play, *Doctor Faustus*?" I asked Kaz. "The man with the devil on one shoulder and the angel on the other?"

Kaz shook his head. He had slowed the car considerably.

"Okay, or like Fred Flintstone, who had the angel Fred on one shoulder and the devil Fred on the other? Groening did the same thing with Homer Simpson?"

Kaz said nothing.

"It's like that. That angel/devil duo is meant, in ancient and modern media, to represent good and evil. Conscience and temptation. Each of these exists in every person and are often at odds. I'm not crazy, I just… Both those voices are in me at all times. Quite loudly and literally."

Except they're actually there. Friend and Trebor. Mom and Dad in direct contradiction. And sometimes they manifest in bigger ways than noise.

"And you talk back to these voices?" he asked.

"I didn't say I was all the way sane," I said, attempting to joke.

"Who is, I suppose," he said while attempting—and failing—to smile. "Do these voices ever…tell you to do things?"

They don't tell me. I just do.

Our speed had picked back up again, but nowhere near as fast as we'd been going when I left my apartment.

"Empusa," I said. "You're uncomfortable around her."

"She's unpleasant," he said. "But she's a decent cop.

Hasn't done anything wrong. She's just…unsettling."

"You seemed pretty uncomfortable."

He gritted his teeth. "We're here," he said.

He didn't need to tell me. As soon as we turned onto the lane leading into a little trailer park, he red and blue lights flashing everywhere were hard to miss. Again, a plethora of cops, black vans, yellow tape—a crime scene.

"Not again," I said.

"Again," he confirmed.

We got out of the car at the same time, but he walked in front of me, ducking us under the crime scene tape wrapped around the perimeter of the fourth trailer in.

"Is this okay, you marching me through crime scenes?" I asked.

The sea of cops and investigators parted as Kaz and I went up the creaky steps and onto the porch of the trailer. I tried not to react to the painting on the door—three hearts squished together, blood drooling down, jagged roots like veins. And another addition to this one: a branch growing out of the middle heart, shooting up above all three and sprouting red leaves that canopied all three hearts like an umbrella.

"Still unfamiliar?" he asked.

I didn't answer.

He handed me a pair of crime scene booties that I slipped over my Converse, and a pair of black latex gloves that were too big. Once we were all geared up, we went inside the trailer, his torch leading the way. He barked at everyone to give him a minute, and people scattered like roaches in his torch beam.

I've never experienced a worse smell, and I'd recently rummaged in a dumpster containing a dying-to-dead fentanyl addict. The inside of the trailer smelled like stale booze and cigarette smoke, urine and feces, and old vomit. There was a medley of food smells, too, but I consciously didn't attempt to decipher those.

"Here," Kaz said, handing me a tub of Vaporub to smear under my nose.

I did, but it didn't help the stench. Now all I was smelling was a minty version of Trebor's semen.

We passed through the living room and kitchen, which was like an episode of *Hoarders*. Hundreds of magazines and newspapers were in piles against the wall, and stacks of takeaway containers and pizza boxes littered almost every centimeter of the carpet. I honed in on a half-open box of pizza and the family of maggots dining on solidified grease that had pooled in the curl of a pepperoni. They squirmed, and my blood squirmed at the sight, and it felt like maggots were squirming on my gums and in between my teeth.

I stared ahead at only Kaz's back. We passed a bedroom and a bathroom, but I didn't look inside. Whatever was in there stank and was rotten, and I had no need to see any more nastiness. Besides, I suspected I'd get an eye-full once we reached our destination.

"Don't touch anything," he said, as if I needed to be told. As if there was anything within me that wanted contact with any part of this mess.

We crossed the threshold into the master bedroom at the end of the narrow hall. He walked inside and stared at me and only me.

I knew why. He couldn't view the scene again. And he was watching me, searching for my reaction.

I didn't have one yet. I didn't know what to think or how to feel about the man on the bed. He was naked atop a pair of fence planks that had been nailed together in a cross. Crude antique nails had been pounded through his ankles and one through each wrist.

CRUCIFIED, Trebor said.

"I fucking know," I answered.

Kaz flinched at my voice.

"Sorry," I said.

"Not me," he said.

"No. Not you."

I shifted my attention to the man. His genitals had been removed, and a gash had been sawed between his legs from asshole to bellybutton. The severed shaft had been used to craft a crude labia and vulva that had been sewn to his body using twine. There was something poking out of the newly constructed genitalia, so I took a step forward to have a closer look.

"Don't touch," Kaz reminded me.

I touched. Ever so softly, I folded back one of the lips and revealed the hidden secret within. A dead mouse poking out of this new vagina.

"Don't touch," Kaz barked, but he didn't stop me.

I let the flap fall back into place and had a quick glance over the rest of the body. The eyes had been removed, and the testicles had been julienned and placed atop the man's head like bloody ringlets.

"These crimes are escalating," I said.

"I'd say," Kaz said.

The art had progressed, too. Painted above the bed on the wainscoting was the trio of squeezed hearts, blood drooling down into roots, the tree growing out of the middle heart. But now the middle heart was the same size as the other two, and the tree had grown, its branches fully encircling and sealing the hearts in its perimeter. And there were more leaves, red, feathered…

I took a step towards the wall, reached out a finger, and touched the leaves of the tree.

"Feathers," I said.

They were actual feathers, red as fresh blood, making up the leaves of the tree.

"Anna," Kaz said.

"I know. No touching."

"The cross," he said.

"I know, I know," I said. "He's crucified."

"The initialism."

Confused, I looked at the man on the cross, then at the cross itself and the jagged piece of wood acting as a sign nailed just above the man's head.

In a church, the initialization would be INRI—Iesus Nazarenus, Rex Iudaeorum in Latin. English translation: Jesus the Nazarene, King of the Jews. This plaque read something different—letters carved into the wood and fingerpainted blood over the gouges.

HTRB

"Do you know what that stands for?" Kaz asked.

I did.

I didn't want to say it aloud, to admit that I had knowledge of this atrocity, but my voice came out, regardless. And it was *my* voice, albeit a trio with Trebor's baritone growl and Mom's saccharine soprano.

"Halfbreed, tainted, rotten bitch."

The phrase hung like smog in the air, pausing time, ceasing motion. Kaz bit his lip. Tears rolled down my face. I looked at my hands, which were now held by Friend, our palms pressed together. She kissed me on the forehead before releasing my hands and dissipating like smoke, leaving me there with bloody palms.

"Anna," Kaz said. "I hate this. I hate to do this."

Friend had bloodied my hands again. How could Kaz still be on my side? I only touched the folds of that vagina with my fingertips, only ran a single finger over the blood. My hands were covered, but not from this, not—

"I didn't," I said.

"Anna," Kaz said. He gently grasped my wrist in his hand and turned me towards the wall. "You are under arrest for—"

I didn't hear much else except for the click of the handcuffs when they clasped my wrists. The pressure of the cold metal caused gooseflesh to rise on my arms as he nudged me back down the hallway, past the spoiled food and maggots in the living room. All those tiny bugs were laughing at me with their mouths full of rotten meat as I passed through the front door, across the yard, paraded by a myriad law enforcement and investigative staff, and ducked into the back of a cruiser that wasn't Kaz's. I could still hear the bug's laughter when he shut the car door.

Chapter Nineteen

The jail cell was cold. And no one was telling me anything. Though I supposed there was nothing to tell. I was being charged with murder. Murders, probably. I had arrived at the station in the middle of the night, and the cop shop was crawling with drunks, streetwalkers, and bar brawlers. It had been so loud, and so smelly, and the woman at the desk had droned in a monotone spiel that I didn't catch one word of. I was being booked, and I'd spend the rest of the night in the cell block until the morning when they could sort out where I was going.

I thought of evidence. Of possibilities. The man in the dumpster, the woman at the grocery store, my upstairs neighbour, the trailer park Jesus. All that evidence they'd have to sift through—fingerprints, DNA, alibis, cameras. So many things they could use to prove it was me.

Was it me?

I didn't know. But it sure involved me. I didn't begrudge Kaz arresting me. How could he not? He wasn't cruel, and he wasn't angry, and the poor bloke seemed just as confused as

I was.

I don't black out. I hadn't. Maybe once or twice back at Eden's Edge, but I didn't lose any time. I just paused a moment to look behind a veil. It was a huge leap to assume I'd tortured, murdered, and created life-sized dioramas without remembering a good goddamn thing. I thought of Patrick and Robbie in the alley behind the Crown and Anchor. I'd killed them. Slaughtered them and consumed the evidence. But I remembered doing that.

Friend sat outside my cell, her arms and legs spread through the bars. I would sit with her eventually, but right then, I wanted to pace. Movement kept panic from settling in. Like a caged animal, I paced, watching my feet. Other people were in the cell block, but I had my own cell. Judging by its size, it was meant for more than just one person, but thankfully I was the only one confined there. There were three cells in all, and mine was in the middle. The cells on either side of me did contain people, but I refused to look. There were quiet, muted conversations, the clearing of throats, soft crying. Men and women both, if I was hearing correctly.

I wondered where they'd send me. Crimes like mine involved max security and a lifetime sentence, I suspected.

Is this it?

Is this my end?

I had no one in my life. I knew nothing of lawyers or courts. What would happen to my apartment and all my stuff? This was just like when Mom and I fled our home and wound up in Eden's Edge. One life ended and another began. We'd brought the bare minimum—clothes, some books, and a few mementos. I left Eden's Edge with less—the clothes on my back and no Mom. Now I didn't even have my freedom.

I guess this was my new life. Caged. Probably for the best. Now it really would be a matter of waiting to die, and for not the first time, I considered expediting the process.

Someone in the cell beside me was pacing now. Their feet passed as I came to the corner of my cell. Not wanting to talk to anyone, I moved back the other way. There were feet there, too. My cell was only so big, and I had run out of spaces to be alone. I opted to take a seat on the long bench against the back wall. I rested my head against the cinderblocks and closed my eyes.

Fire. The ash was slick on my tongue, the heat sizzled my flesh. I truly believed the jail and the entire basement were going up in flames until I opened my eyes. There was fire, but it was on one side of the basement only. The cell to my left was burning. The steel seating and latrines were covered in a sheet of flames, and the black floor glowed and flickered like charcoals. The bars were white hot from the heat, and steam was rising from the occupant's flesh.

The occupants. They were beasts—all rough skin, forked tongues, swishing tails. Half a dozen demons stalked around the cell, their eyes bleeding red, their thick chests swelling with muscle. When they'd pass too close, they'd bite off flesh or gouge each other with jagged talons. They snorted like hogs and wheezed like hyenas, their manic noise crescendoing as the flames burned brighter.

In the cell on the other side of me was the cool embrace of fauna and flora. The cell floor was loam, the furniture stone. A cool black fog speckled with stars lined the ceiling. It smelled of trees, moss, and dirt, with the pungent aroma of animal markings and decay. The feminine figures within were all entwined, pirouetting around the cell like bones connected by lace. Some had heads, some didn't, all had black eyes, wide mouths, and translucent flesh. There were markings scratched on their arms, chests, and stomachs, symbols and language foreign to me. They danced, howled, and dirt spilled out of their mouths as they burst into song, their feet drumming the soil beneath their bare feet.

I sat on the floor in the middle of my cell. I allowed Friend to reach through the bars to hold me as the heat on my left scorched me while the other side soothed me. On the left there was the percussive pacing of hooves, and on the right, the soft patter of bare feet. Ahead was the tapping of something closer to sane. Shoes.

"Anna."

"Liza." I stood from Friend's grasp and took the hands of my human friend on the free side of the bars.

"What are you doing here?" I asked.

"Kaz called me," Liza said. "I came straight away."

"You shouldn't have," I said. "This is my mess."

"This isn't yours," Liza said. "You did nothing to cause any of this."

"I'm involved," I said. "Somehow."

"We'll figure it out." She gave my hands a squeeze.

We.

Why was she here? If I was her, I'd run far, far away, out of the line of tragedy.

"I tried to post bail," she said. "To get you out. I would've taken a loan, anything. But it isn't an issue of money."

"No," I said. "Quadruple homicide usually doesn't come with get-out-of-jail-free cards, no matter how much money you toss at it."

"There has to be a way," she said.

"And what?" I said. "Get out and wait to go to trial? Wait to come back and have to defend myself, explain this insanity? They might not have any concrete evidence, but to a jury, it sure seems suspicious, doesn't it?"

"All we need is doubt," she said.

"And what do I say? I've been hiding all these years. If they start snooping, start seeing connections—there are only a couple outs. Jail or institutionalized. I'm not sure what's worse."

"One and the same," she said quietly.

She was going to cry if she spoke another word. Her eyes

were filled to the brim with fat tears, and her lip was trembling. The last thing I wanted for her was more hurt, more trauma. I looked to my left at the demons stalking us, and to the right at the root witches waltzing, howling, and caressing each other.

And me, right in the middle.

"I can get out," I said.

"What?"

We stared into each other's eyes. I let my words sink in and watched her face morph from confused, to realization, to horror, then acceptance.

"Do you know…how?"

I shrugged. "Can't hurt to try, right?" I said.

"What do you need me to do?" she asked.

"Wait for me," I said.

"Of course," she said. "Where?"

I didn't know. They'd be searching for me everywhere.

"We can leave," she said.

"I don't expect you to do this," I said. "To leave your life."

"What life?" she asked.

The guard at the door shifted his weight, and the armies around me squalled and twittered like someone had rattled their cages.

"He'll show you out, yes?" I asked.

"I imagine so."

"Drive. Down the block and around the corner. That old Phō restaurant."

She didn't ask questions but wasn't sure, though. She held onto my hands, squeezing harder instead of releasing me. She would have kept holding me if the guard had not banged on the bars with his baton.

"Finish up," he barked.

Liza dropped my hands and left.

"Five minutes," I mouthed, unsure if that was even possible.

I waited for her and the guard to disappear up the stairs. Once I could no longer see or hear them, I went to Friend, who was hanging upside down by her feet from the ceiling.

"Help me," I said.

She knew what to do. She sucked in air and slithered through the bars, then stood behind me and pressed into me.

Banshees wailing and chainsaws destroying. That's the only way to describe the sound in that basement when the hordes of impossible things around me freaked out, jumping, smashing, and beating on the bars. I ripped the cell door off with little effort and decided this rowdy bunch could help. I tore off the witches's door, then the demons's, and they all started slashing, biting, and kicking at each other.

"Enough," I commanded in a voice both masculine and feminine, strong and wise.

They didn't silence or still, but they quit trying to slaughter each other. We all moved up the stairs as a pack, my horde in tow, and when we got to the door to the police station proper at the top, I opened it and let them through first.

I'm not sure what everyone saw. I suspected they didn't see witches and demons. But they did see the chaos that blew through the reception area like a tornado. Paper whorled to the ceiling, desks tremored and flipped, and the glass smashed out of the windows. People were running and screaming, officers were on their radios, while people shouted theories:

"Storm."

"Tornado."

"Earthquake."

"Aliens."

As chaos consumed the office, I reverted to plain ole Anna. Friend and I moseyed out the front door undetected. I walked, calm and controlled, down the street, and around the corner to the parking lot of the Phō restaurant where Liza was waiting for me in a little black sedan. I opened the back door first, letting Friend inside before I crawled in the passenger seat.

"Let's go," I said.

She was staring at the backseat.

"She's there," I said.

Liza looked at me. "Okay," she said.

And she drove until the city lights disappeared, and stars appeared.

Chapter Twenty

Liza looked like she was fighting to stay awake, so I offered more than once to drive. She declined. I don't know if it's because she didn't fully trust me, or because she was being kind. Or maybe she knew that I didn't have a driver's license, had only been behind the wheel a handful of times, and never for more than a few meters. Thank goodness we weren't too far from the ferry terminal. We reached there just as dawn started yawning across the sky.

I loved morning skies. I'd forgotten how beautiful they were, blooming from pink to soft blue. This day had a touch of storm about it, leaving the sky a darker grey as it heated from pink to orange before clouding over. I didn't know where we were headed; we hadn't talked about it in the brief time we had in the basement of the police station. And since we'd gotten in the car, we'd uttered less than a few sentences. It wasn't tense. It was a comfortable, exhausted silence that didn't need to be filled. I apologized, and she told me it was okay. It wasn't my fault. I cried, and she cried too, and together we cried for a spell before the rumbling of the road lulled us into silence. I took full advantage. I didn't contemplate or problem solve. I just closed my eyes, listened to the wheels on the asphalt. Once we were out of the city, cracked my window and breathed in deep the scent of nature.

I tried to remember the last time I'd left the concrete jungle to feel my feet in the dirt. Not since they picked me up as a child. They lifted me from the backyard of my home in Eden's Edge, prying my feet from the dirt like a tongue from a frozen pole, and placed me in the back of that cruiser. My feet had seen the floors of hospitals, courthouses, foster homes, and the street. Back alleys, strange bedrooms, shelters. But never back in the dirt. Not since that night.

When we reached the ferry terminal, Liza bought our tickets and came back out to the parking lot with a sheepish gait. "We board in half an hour," she said. "Throw this on."

It was a UBC hoodie, and not new from the look of it. I stepped out of the car to slip it on while she gathered things from the backseat.

"Are we leaving the car?" I asked.

"Yeah," she said.

When we ran from our old life to our new, we'd left our car beside the dumpster at the little diner where I first saw Friend's artwork. She was New Friend at the time. Brand New Friend.

"I think it's best," Liza said.

"I know," I said. "Thank you."

"Thank you," she said.

"For what?" I asked.

"For letting me into your life again."

"Don't thank me for the mess I've made for you."

Liza took my face in her hands. "You've made no mess. And we face whatever this is together. It's ours."

For whatever little time I had, I was happy Liza was with me. I didn't know if the rest of my life would be spent in jail, dead, or worse, but I was glad for this moment with her. I adored her we first met in the library at Eden's Edge and our first walk in the cemetery. I felt I had known her for both a minute and an entire lifetime, both then and now.

In the blink of an eye, we were off, pulling away from the dock and beginning our journey from Tsawwassen to Swartz Bay. I didn't question our destination, though I would have chosen the northern part of the island with fewer people, fewer roads, and less law enforcement. But Victoria was beautiful. Mom, Dad, and I had been there plenty of times when I was a child. We played on the beach, watched Orcas off the coast, visited the wax museum in the harbour, and ended the day enjoying fireworks at Bouchard Gardens.

Natural beauty was ubiquitous on the island: ocean, rock, earth, and sky. I wished all the people would dissolve and leave me alone there, segregated from the world, the hurt, and the world beyond—no people, no witches, no demons, nothing.

I wondered how my end would reach me. Where it would be and who I'd be with.

"You want to come inside?" Liza asked as we picked up speed.

"No," I said.

I wanted to stay outside with the salt air whipping my face, listening to the slap of waves against the hull of the ferry.

"Would you like to be alone?" she asked.

"I would," I said.

"Okay," she said, soft and accepting. "I'll go grab us some coffees. Food?"

"No thanks," I said.

Liza disappeared behind me. The day was overcast and a touch blustery, so I was one of a few numb stragglers that opted to stay outside on the deck. A lone gentleman was on the rail across from me, and a woman was seated on a bench, trying to wrangle the pages of her paperback. I turned my attention to the waves, watching them rise and froth. The water was crystal behind the roll, and I tracked the surface, searching.

"There," the man across the way shouted. "Miss?"

I looked at him, at his face covered in child-like wonder.

"It's there!" he repeated, pointing at the open ocean.

There it was indeed. A black fin breached the water like a wave. And another. An entire pod of Orcas approached our boat. I allowed myself to feel amazement and watch in wonder as they drew closer, going over and under the blue with each swell. Behind them, rolling off the inlet hills, was a black and smoky fog that seemed to chase the whales.

"Foggy day?" I said, more a question than a statement.

But the man didn't hear me. Of course he didn't, not over the sound of the ship cutting through the water and the wind whipping across our ears. He was so enraptured by the whales I doubt he would've heard the ship's foghorn, should it blow.

The fog was rolling in faster, gaining on the whales. I was anxious for them, as if the fog intended to swallow them. I had been on this ocean and this ferry a great many times and had never seen fog like this. It was more like ash—the silt we had to brush off Mom's car after Mount Saint Helen's had erupted when I was barely two. My breath grew shallow as the fog approached. I tugged at the collar of my hoodie, tried to breathe deep, but my lungs contracted as the fog reached the many obsidian fins racing through the drink. Then they were drowning, those whales. Their noise rattled in my head; the racket of their screaming, gasping, dying was enough to drive me to jump in the frigid waters with them. I leaned over the edge to see, as they went under the ferry in many bits: fins, eyes, and tails detached from bodies. The salt water was warm and red, an ocean of blood filled with gristle and bone. It sprayed onto my face, coating my eyes, and soon, everything was crimson, and tainted...

... ROTTEN BITCH...

…I wailed into the bay, and the gulls and orcas bellowed with me. I wiped my hands over my face but couldn't clean the blood, so I ran for the back of the ship. I didn't know what I expected to find there, but I needed to be away from the front, from the fog that was coming to take me, too.

Behind the ferry, it was blue and calm. There was no fog, and the whales swam safely clear of the vessel. The mist of sea spray cleansed the blood from my face and eyes, and I looked to Vancouver proper, which was a speck on a faraway shore, and realized I'd left the calm behind. Peeking around the corner of the cabin, I saw red, and the black fog, and knew that we were going towards pain, death, and suffering, not away from it.

"You good?" Liza was standing there like she'd always been there, but she must have gone inside because she was brandishing two steaming cups of coffee.

"I'm never going to be okay again," I said. "I'm not sure I've ever, ever been okay."

The darkness in me was overflowing into reality. And evil awaited. Or maybe I was bringing evil with me as we traveled.

She placed the coffee in my hand. She didn't try to argue and tell me I was wrong, or that everything was going to be okay. She just held me, sipped her coffee, encouraged me to drink mine, and walked with me to the front of the ferry to watch the approach to our impending doom.

Chapter Twenty-One

I wondered what we'd do once we got to the island. Certainly nothing was in walking distance, and I wasn't sure we had money to hail a cab or rent a car. But Liza had everything taken care of.

"I did it from the ferry," she said as she stuck the keys into an old blue Toyota Corolla station wagon. "Rent-a-wreck."

We got in, and the old car groaned under our weight.

"Well," she said. "It's functional. Hopefully this wreck will get us at least a few meters."

I couldn't help but laugh. We laughed so hard we cried, even harder when the Corolla backfired when we pulled out of the ferry terminal. My heart…

…Hearts…

…Smiled as we headed towards Victoria. I could almost taste the seafood on the patios on the inner harbour. Maybe we'd even go for tea at The Empress. That climbing ivy smelled so lovely in the fall.

But we didn't stay on the highway for long. Liza was watching her phone, which directed her north.

"You look disappointed," she said once we were two songs deep up the two-lane secondary highway.

"I am a bit," I said. "Assumption."

"You assumed we were going to the city?" she asked.

"No," I said. "I guess 'hoped' is the word. The city is a risk."

"Too populated," she said.

"Yeah," I agreed. "So…will you tell me where we're going?"

"I don't really know," she admitted. "Just up and away."

"Up and away," I parroted.

So, we drove up and away from the ferry terminal, Victoria, and all the murderous fog and dead whales. We sped by lots of cottages and motels that were barely visible in the now full-night. I wondered if we'd drive all the way up and into the ocean, along the ocean floor beside the Haida Gwaii until we found a suitable place for a watery grave.

Liza touched the brakes, and I gasped.

"No?" she said. "Somewhere else?"

She was slowing the car as we approached a half-overgrown turn off the side of the highway. "It's a campground," she said. "Might be our safest bet."

"Pretty cold," I said, but I didn't mind. I was numb anyway.

"There are cabins," Liza said. "I didn't book ahead, but it's off season, and—"

"It's good," I said.

Even if it wasn't, I needed to stop moving. I wanted to be still, preferably with my head on a pillow and my eyes closed. Hell, even on the cold, hard ground, if that's all that was available.

We crawled up a single-lane gravel road beneath a thick canopy of cedars until the mouth of the forest opened to a cozy campground. There was a space for tenters on one side, which was completely empty, and four log cabins on the other side. In the middle was a wooden longhouse with string lights hanging from the eves that washed the ground in a golden glow.

We pulled into a parking spot at the front door and went inside. A little bell rang, announcing our arrival. A portly woman with bright red lips and a white smile came out from a back room to greet us.

"Hello, folks," she chimed. "Rollin up awful late."

"Sorry, we just got off the ferry," I said. "Didn't quite know where we were headed."

"Few things," the woman said. "Name's Marie."

"Hello," Liza said. "I'm Liza."

"Laveau?" I asked.

Marie and Liza looked at me. I wondered how many heads I'd grown this time.

"The witch," I said. "Voodoo soothsayer. You share a name with her, is all."

Liza's smile warmed my entire soul. "She's always had a thing for witches," she said.

"Well," Marie said, "that's lovely. Do you have a name?"

"Anna," I said.

"Aye, Anna," Marie said like two-tones in a scale. "A beautiful name. T'was a famous Anna, you know. Daughter of the Swedish witch, Malin Matsdotter."

"Precisely who Mom named me after," I said.

Someone like me. Who knew these things. My face ached from smiling before I realized how odd this all was. I was going to ask how Marie knew that, but she didn't give me the chance.

"And second," Marie said, "because I was counting if you remember."

She paused for us to give her confirmation that we were paying attention. We nodded in unison like the schoolchildren we once were.

"And second, there's no need for sorrys around here,"

Marie said. "You could roll up here at ten past the witching hour and I'd greet you with a smile and a tea. And mean every drop of it."

"That's kind of you," I said.

"I must say, ladies, that you could've saved yourself some hours. Where'd you come from?"

"Vancouver," I said.

Liza shot me a harsh look.

Oh, right, we're on the run.

I should be used to being on the run by now.

Marie studied us. First Liza, then me, checking us out from head to toe before taking a gander at our wreck of a rental car.

"Listen here, lovelies," Marie said. "Don't care where you came from, don't care where you're going. What I care is that you're here, safe, comfortable, and as close to happy as you can be at this very moment in time."

The words were magic. My anxiety and tension were butter melting off and pooling on the ground.

"What I meant by asking you where you came from is that there's a ferry comes in near to here. There was no need of you driving all the way up from the south island. But you're here now, and you're tired, so let's get you squared away."

"Do you have any cabins available?" Liza asked.

"I wouldn't let you tent," Marie said. "Colder 'n a witch's tit out there."

She waddled behind the counter in the center of the longhouse. After rummaging through some boxes, she brought out an old, rusted key.

"I'll putcha in cabin four," she said. "She's a lovely one. Not our biggest, but our most interesting. Decorated her up myself. And she's got the biggest haul of books on her shelves. Either of you like to read?"

How long had it been since I'd read a book?

So long.

Since Mom died.

"I love reading," I said. "I used to be a complete bookworm."

Marie's eyes turned sad. "What happened, dear?"

"Life," I said.

Quiet wrapped around us. The old cuckoo clock tick-tick-ticked above the fireplace on the far wall. Wind rustled the branches outside, and in the distance, a frog croaked its midnight melody.

"Go on, then," Marie said. "Go get yourselves some shut eye. And take this with you."

She came around the counter with a paper bag in her hand and placed it in my arms. A quick glance was all I needed to see the magic within—fresh bread, cheese, smoked fish, red wine.

"You really don't have to," I said.

"No," she said. "I want to."

Liza pulled out a credit card.

Marie waved it away. "Worry about it upon your departure, young lady."

"What?" Liza said. "Really?"

"You's have enough to worry about, it would seem. You go on now, have yourself a feed and a sleep, and we'll reconvene in the morning. I cook a mean Eggs Benedict with salmon. I'll fire up the stove when I see your outside light come on."

Lisa was going to argue, and I should have, but neither of us did. I took her hand, and we got in our car and moved it to its new spot in front of cabin four.

Chapter Twenty-Two

Liza and I ate all that cheese and fish and drank all that wine. We chatted, cried, and laughed.

We talked about the library, the woods, and the cemetery. We reminisced about our time before Eden's Edge, when we were little girls. I enjoyed books, gardening, and animals. She loved sports and watching scary movies in the dark. I wondered if I could do that. My life was basically a scary movie, so I shouldn't be frightened by monsters on screen.

Are the monsters ever scared?

Liza checked out the cupboards and found three more bottles of wine. As she poured, I noticed there was no dust on the bottles.

Thank you, Marie.

"Do you think about them?" I asked.

"Who?" Liza asked said as she sat beside me on the fluffy rug in front of the crackling fireplace.

I could barely say their names. "Mary," I whispered. "And Laz."

Her eyes were dark and danced with fire as she watched the flame. "Yeah," was all she said.

The snap Laz's neck made when Bobby Pickton cranked it to the side was a sound I heard every time a door closed, someone dropped something on the floor, or my joints popped.

Sometimes, when I looked in the mirror, I saw Mary's eyes in my sockets as she watched me out that car window, pleading with me to save her as Bobby drove her off to fuck knows what torture.

"I feel so guilty," I said.

"Why?" Liza asked.

"I could have saved them," I said. A thick lump formed in my throat.

"How?" she asked.

"Like I saved you," I said.

She looked away from the fire, at me, and put her hand on my knee. "You didn't know," she said. "What you…could do. What you were."

"I still don't know what I am," I said.

Demon. Witch. Half-and-half. I was an impossible thing with no place, no control, and no direction.

HALF-BREED TAINTED ROTTEN BITCH.

"Please stop," I said to Trebor.

I cupped my ears, but it only served to trap his voice in my skull, making it louder and more intimate.

Liza gently pulled my hands away from my ears. "You saved me," she said.

Trebor fell silent.

"And I know what you are," she said.

She had seen me transform right before I killed Bobby. She saw what I was then, what I was capable of, and the stench of fear like sour meat wafted from her pores. What would she think of me now? What would she think if she saw Friend and I in that alley, all contorted bones and swollen black muscles, consuming a pair of humans?

"What am I?" I dared to ask.

Liza took my hands and knelt in front of me. Her breath was sweet in my mouth, like cotton candy.

"You are Anna," she said.

Nothing else mattered in that moment. There was us and cabin number four with its crackling fire and the safety of its log walls. Only Liza and I ran through the woods as children, our hair flying behind us like veils, our laughter chiming in unison with the birdsong. Liza and I on our backs in the cemetery, looking up at the fluffy clouds, then the twinkling stars meeting the pink of dawn.

The touch of her mouth on mine brought me back to the present. Her lips were as sweet as her breath. I don't know who leaned in, but our lips were pressed together, soft at first then firm and hungry. Her tongue parted my lips and entered my mouth as I threaded my fingers through her hair while holding her face on mine. Her fingers crawled to the hem of my shirt. She lifted it over my head, while I unbuttoned her shirt and let it slide off her shoulders. We kissed again, undoing each other's bras, which fell to the floor like silk.

Liza was the most beautiful thing I'd ever seen: golden skin, dark nipples, raven-black hair flowing and coiling down, touching her stomach. I massaged her breasts in my hands until her head dropped back, then I took a nipple into my mouth, circling it with my tongue until it was erect, then moved to the other. She pressed into me, rubbing her breasts up and down my face, then burying her face in mine while pinching my nipples and twirling them between her beautiful fingers.

We fumbled, rubbed, and groped our way out of our pants. She took off her panties, and I went to take mine off, but she stopped me.

"Let me," she said. Her smoky words enticed gooseflesh to rise over my entire body.

I wanted to protest, to pleasure her. But I didn't. I allowed myself to lay back on that carpet, the soft fibers warm on my back while her hands were cool on my body. I closed my eyes. I wanted only to feel—not to see, to hear, to smell. I focused on the sensation of my panties sliding down my legs and off my feet, on her gently opening my legs with her palms, on her hair tickling the insides of my thighs. Her fingers massaged the outside of my labia, and my body clenched. I wanted to scream, to beg for more, but she was slow and soft. She kissed my vulva, then, like she had done with my mouth, parted me with her tongue. She held tight to my ass as she licked my clit, slow, firm, and my head went light. She moved faster, harder. When her left hand slid over my thigh and between my legs, tumbled, losing control, and when she penetrated me with one, two, three fingers, thrusting and licking, moaning into me, my whole body tensed. I exploded into a climax so violent I could barely stand it. I focused on her face between my legs, her fingers inside me in a pleasure so intense I cried, screamed, and laughed.

I tried to wriggle out from under her. I wanted to taste her, to feel her on the inside, to crawl right under her skin, but she wasn't done. She rolled me onto my knees and rubbed my clit with her palm as she used her other hand to penetrate me, pumping me to climax again until my thighs and the rug at my knees were soaked.

I rolled onto my back and guided her on top of me until she was straddling my face. I plunged my tongue inside her while she grinded against me. I coaxed her to climax with my thumb and she filled my mouth. I thought of the sea, of the salt water, of Liza and I, hands entwined, the ocean in front of us, the sand on our bare skin.

She slid down and collapsed on top of me. Our breasts squished together, our limbs entwined so the wetness between our legs came to rest on each other's thighs. We came once more, grinding against each other like that. Then she kissed me. I kissed her.

There was nothing else but us, the fire, and the ocean.

Chapter Twenty-Three

My body was still pulsing and tender when I woke in the middle of the night. The fire had died, leaving simmering embers in place of full logs, so the chill was what must have coaxed me awake. I was freezing. I peeled myself away from Liza, who was sleeping soundly; the cutest little puffs of air were passing her lips as she slept. I took care to place her leg gently on the carpet as I lifted it off me and stood. I went to the kitchen, quietly wet a washcloth, and washed away the stickiness on my body and between my legs. By then, I was shivering violently from the cold, so I put my clothes on, including the UBC hoodie, and wrapped myself in a Hudson Bay blanket I found in the linen closet.

Liza would be cold when she woke up, even if she slept in late. I checked the log basket for more wood, but we'd burned every piece through the night. When we'd arrived, I noticed piles of firewood stacked against the longhouse. I decided to sneak out and go grab some so Liza would be warm when she woke.

The darkness of the night was oppressive, and the lights around the longhouse were warm but faint, offering very little visibility as I walked over to get some wood. I looked at the other cabins, wondering if anyone else was spending the night. There were no other cars, but that didn't mean anything. People could have taxied from the Northern Terminal Ferry.

It was pretty quiet, though. Unnerving. There were no sounds of forest or creature, which struck me as odd this deep into the woods. There wasn't an off switch for nature. Critters of all flavours should have been scuttling around, enjoying their nightly escapades, but not so much as a breeze rustled those trees.

All the lights were on in the longhouse. I debated about just scooping up an armload of wood and skulking back to cabin four, but I thought better of it. Marie had shown us great kindness by letting us stay without so much as evidence of a means of payment. I didn't want to steal wood from her stash without asking first.

The little bell chimed, announcing my arrival.

"Do come in," Marie chirped from behind the aisles in the back.

"Hi Marie," I called out. "It's Anna." I felt the need to acknowledge it was me, especially this isolated in the woods. Was Marie alone out here?

"I know it's you," Marie chuffed.

There were no windows along the sides of the longhouse, and none in the back. There was no way she could have seen me walk up.

Cameras.

NEIN. Trebor laughed.

"Shut up," I whispered.

"Pardon?"

"Not you," I said to Marie.

She appeared from between the aisles and made her way

up to the counter.

"I was just hoping to grab some wood," I said. "Fire went out."

"Ah yes, of course, take what you need," she said. "Kind of you to ask, but you are welcome to anything on the property."

Her ruby lips were curved to her cheeks, and her eyes twinkled. She was joy in the flesh.

"You are so kind," I said. "Thank you. Truly."

"Is that all?" she asked.

"Um…"

"The firewood," she said. "Is that all you need?"

I hesitated. Thoughts of breakfast came to mind—eggs, bacon, coffee.

"Not food, dear," she said.

My heart hitched in my chest. She was reading my mind? "Who are… What…" I stammered.

"Oh, I didn't mean to shock you, my dearie," she said. "But I thought there'd be no shocking the likes of you."

She dug around behind the counter, looking through drawers until she found a key ring with a dozen keys dangling off.

"The likes of me?" I asked.

She rose from behind the counter with that smile, her gleaming, ruby lips bared to flash her toothy smile. "Come," she said.

With that, she waddled out the door. The little bell rang, and it sounded like a voice instructing me to come. So I did. She walked down the lane in front of cabin one, cabin two, cabin three, then cabin four. She didn't stop at the edge of the property but rather continued on into the trees and down a dirt trail that was only millimeters wider than she was.

"You warm enough, hon?" she called back.

I wrapped my blanket tighter around me, but no amount of fabric or fire would warm the chill in my bones.

"I gots me enough layers of blubber to keep me going here in the cold season," she said with a chuckle. "Plus, I like the outdoors at the end of the year cycle. The fires of autumn and the glitter of winter."

Why was I following this woman? Why was I traipsing around in the dark woods, all alone, where no light and no sounds existed? Hadn't I seen enough death, murder, and afterlife? Why would I put myself in this situation?

I had no fear. And with good reason. There was nothing here, in this spot, in this moment, to be afraid of. I could hold my own against a little old lady.

We reached a small clearing with a tiny cottage adorned with the same string lights as the longhouse.

"This be my home," she said with pride. "Not much, but it's my everything."

It was quaint but complex: intricate decorations, ornate carved logs for walls, a towering totem pole with a Canadian flag flying from the tallest totem. There was no grass; the entire yard was a garden filled with bushes, flowers, vegetables, and weeds. It was teeming with life and colour, sounds and smells.

"You like it?" she asked.

I did. I really did. I looked at her to tell her so, but my breath was stolen by the headless crimson bird perched on her shoulder.

"Erinyes," I said.

"Yes," Marie said. "She arrived just ahead of you. Jolly little bird, isn't she?"

"She was…"

"Still is your mom's, dear. Always will be." Marie pulled the door to the cottage open, and it creaked like an old woman's knees. "Come on in for a cuppa, honey," she said. "We have much to discuss."

A stranger's house, in the middle of the woods, in the middle of the night. I might not have gone in if it wasn't for

Erinyes on her shoulder, and Gus scurrying in between her feet, and the glow of warmth reaching for me like familiar hands from inside.

Chapter Twenty-Four

The tea was Rooibos—mine's and mom's favourite. Erinyes had perched atop the hearth with Gus at her side. The two of them were chittering and chattering in their respective languages, telling each other grande stories. Marie sipped her tea from a dainty cup with gold edging while I sucked mine from a blocky mug with the phrase 'I'M A CONSTANT FUCKING DELIGHT' printed on the side. On brand for both of us, I supposed.

"You are a witch," I said.

"Yep," she said.

"I thought I was, too. Once upon a time."

"There's witch in you," she said, nodding to the squirrel and bird on the hearth.

"Among other things," I said.

HUMAN-SHAPED SACK OF MEAT SHIT.

"Fuck you," I said to Trebor.

"Imbecile," Marie said. There was no shock on her face. No judgement.

"You can hear him?" I asked.

"In my way," she said. "His language isn't mine, but I get his sentiment."

I took another mouthful of tea. In another life, another time, I could imagine that this was my mom sitting across from me, her voice a song, her smile a hug. In a way, it was. My mom was here somehow, in this place, in all the leaves, bones, and critters.

"You asked what I needed," I said.

"Aye," Marie said with a nod.

"I don't know what I need," I said.

"You are on the run, yes?" Marie asked. Her eyes were soft. She wasn't accusing or judging.

"Yeah," I admitted.

"From yourself," she said. A statement, not a question. "Hard to outrun your own feet."

"No, there was… People died," I said.

"As people do," she said.

"Not died," I clarified. "Were murdered"

"But they died nonetheless," she said.

"I was arrested," I said. I was ashamed. I'd mostly thought myself to be a good girl. A moral woman. But…

"And there's the meat of it," she said. "Did you do it? The murders?"

"I'm not sure," I said.

She didn't react with shock, horror, or even surprise. She gave me a loving look with kind eyes, patted my leg, and took my empty mug from me. "Take a beat," she said, "while I fetch us a refill."

She disappeared into her kitchen, leaving me alone with Erinyes, Gus, and my thoughts. The most dangerous creature in the room was me and my mind. Flashes of corpses revealed themselves to me when I blinked, and the thoughts of the now-digested meat in my body raised my heart-rate, clenched my lungs. I started panting. Beads of sweat formed on my brow, beneath my breasts, and on my upper lip. I imagined that sweat was glistening fat—the remnants of Robbie Cum Crocs come to accuse me of being the monster that I was.

I stood. Movement was distracting, and distraction tamped panic down deep in my bowels where it belonged. There was no shortage of distracting things in Marie's living room, so I perused the shelves. She had the kind of house I wanted, full of life and experience. There were plants vining up the walls and occupying the corners, knick-knacks on every surface, and remnants of the outside scattered all over the inside—leaves, flowers, bones, shells. I respectfully didn't touch any of it, but I soaked it all in with my eyes. I came to a mortar and pestle on the top of an upright grande in the corner. There were remnants of something crushed within—a fine grey dust that sparkled under her many fairy lights that hung in loops off the ceiling.

"Fly agaric," she said when she came back in the room.

"Pardon?"

"Fly agaric," she repeated. "That's what I dried and crushed in that mortar. It's your typically fairy-tale mushroom—white base, red top with little polka dots. Cute, pretty, and a lunatic of the poison to the mind."

She came over, swiped the dust with her finger, and plunged the dusted finger into her mouth.

"Toxic, you say," I noted.

"Parboiling it twice with water weakens its toxicity and breaks down its psychoactive properties. It becomes passive like chamomile with a little more sparkle, if you know what I mean."

I wished I had learned more from my mom. I remember things like this that she did, the songs she used to hum deep in her throat while she floated around the house, creating, mixing, and growing.

Erinyes flew from the hearth and landed on the edge of the mortar. She bent and fluttered her wings. I realized she was trying to peck at the contents of the bowl. Gus, recognizing her distress, came to the bowl. He swiped a paw over the power and smeared it on Erinyes's exposed neck.

I hadn't noticed Marie disappear deep into the house again. I sat in the old rocking chair and watched tendrils of steam rise from my cup.

"It isn't poisoned," she said when she reappeared once more, this time with a small burlap bag in her hand. "There's no poisoning the likes of you."

"I could never get drunk," I admitted. "Or high. Not for lack of trying, especially during my time on the streets."

"Oh deary," she said as she plucked the mortar and pestle off the shelf and placed it on the coffee table. "You've had a hard go of it."

I nodded. I really had. I didn't even know what not-hard looked like.

She took her place on the couch across from me. She reached into her bag, grabbed four of the little red mushrooms, and plunked them into the mortar. Next, she drew out two shriveled black orbs that looked like rotten grapes.

"Coyote eyes," she said.

"Coyote?"

"Yes, honey. Not easy to come by. There aren't any on the island, you know. They are swarming on the mainland, though. I don't often need them, but I don't feel guilty when I do."

"You killed it?" I said, somehow saddened by that.

"Sure did," she said with pride. "Bare hands, too. Roadkill doesn't have the same effect. They gotta be screaming when they go for this to work."

"For what to work?"

She answered by grinding up the dehydrated eyes with the mushrooms, creating a pasty powder that looked like dried menstrual blood. Once it was all mixed up, she reached in her sack again and pulled out a shot glass and a mini bottle of

Iceberg vodka.

"I can't get drunk," I reminded her. "That will have zero effect."

She poured up the shot and mixed in the red paste, creating a glittering red concoction.

"That's why it's safe," she said. "The fly agaric won't harm you, nor will it make you high, even though I didn't weaken it. What it will do, mixed with the mongrel's eyes, is allow you to see what you need."

She pushed my mug of tea aside and placed the shot glass in its place.

"See what?" I asked.

"What you need to see."

I didn't much care if I died. I had spent all my teens and early adulthood just waiting for it all to be over, so this wasn't something I hadn't considered many a time before. But now, after being with Liza, the feeling of her flesh on mine and our hearts together, I wasn't so sure.

"Drink up," Marie said. "I'll be right here."

Erinyes and Gus had taken their places on either side of the shot glass. They were very still—Gus's eyes laser focused on me, Erinyes's body aimed as if she would be staring at me if she had a head and eyes to do so.

I closed my eyes and poured the liquid down my throat.

"Don't open them until it hits," Marie said.

I didn't know what I was waiting for. I'd never been drunk, or high, and—

Oh.

My head floated off my body like a balloon. I pictured Erinyes, and the headless New Friend of long ago, and wondered if this is what it felt like for them. I tried to touch my neck, but my hands wouldn't work. My head was up and moving around the cottage on its own.

I opened my eyes.

Everything was burning. Not violently, though. Just a

simmering glow of tired embers and shining black ash over every surface. Marie was seated on the couch still, but she was naked, her arms and legs and hair made of clusters of snakes. She smiled, revealing fangs for teeth and a rat snake for a tongue. Her hair was a wild gorgon, snakes fanning out and coiling into iridescent ringlets.

"I knew a bug witch," I said. My voice was laced with helium, high and flighty.

"We are all of nature," she said. "I am sssserpent."

"I am dirt," I said.

Was I? Why did I say that?

"Dirt issss beautiful," she said. "It issss life and growth."

I moved around the cottage, wanted to look at all the things, but everything was covered in ash and dirt. Well, not everything. Some things. Others were glowing in full technicolor.

Erinyes was flaming red. Gus was a deep, ruddy brown the hue of warm chocolate. Marie's snakes shimmered in of the entire rainbow. An object on the piano gleamed in the glow from the fairy lights. I went to it, picked it up.

It was a wine stopper, cabernet sauvignon still dripping from the tip like blood. The top was a beautiful woman, naked, her legs coming together to form the stopper. But her legs…

One was hair-covered with a hoof at the end, the other was brass.

"A shapeshifter," Marie said. "A demonic female with one leg that of a donkey and the other of brass. In folklore, she pursues travelers and eats them."

"That's… odd," I said.

"Recognisssse her aroma? You know her name."

I sniffed the stopper and gagged. It wasn't the sweet tang of wine, but the sharp stench of manure and livestock. There was a distinct undertone as well. Something too clean and too sterile. A hospital.

I thought of the officer with the weird gait and the accusatory eyes. "Empusa," I said.

I dropped the stopper, and it hit the floor with a bang, smashing into a million pieces and jarring me out of my hallucination.

"A demon is after me," I said.

I panicked. I pressed my hand against my chest to slow my heart.

"Now might be the time for your tea, dear," Marie said as she guided me into the rocking chair again.

I refused to sit. I drank the tea standing. It didn't help.

"I'm in danger," I said.

She laughed. It was a joyful, soothing noise, like a child's lullaby. "We're all in danger," she said. "All of us. Always."

"A demon is after me," I said.

"Aye," she said. "Would seem so. But then both sides of the veils have been reaching for you for quite some time, I suppose."

It was true. I'd always been different as a child, but my first strong tangible experience was meeting New Friend in that diner.

The couch creaked when Marie sat, but then it creaked again, twice more.

I didn't want to know who was there with her.

"The mushrooms haven't worn off," I said as I studied the pills of fabric on my pajama bottoms.

"They have," Marie said. "But the mongrel's eyes have not."

I looked up to find her snake-free, but she wasn't alone on that couch. On one side of her was Friend, her head resting on Marie's bosom. On her other side was Trebor, his massive bulk taking up his entire side of the couch and the floor beyond. His snaking cocks wisped their tongues out on Marie's fleshy arm. She pulled off one of her slippers and thwapped that cock on the head, and they all retreated into

Trebor's body.

"Nasty buggers," she said.

"You see?" I asked.

"I see," she said. "I'm old, my girl, and have lived a life. My veil was lifted long ago. Took me a while to decipher what belonged on which side. It was a chore to not react to the spirit world when I was in aisle four of the market, grabbing crisps and pop. Still is, sometimes."

I missed Mom. I needed her here to guide me.

"How did you learn?" I asked.

"I didn't fear it," she said. "I had the women in my life to guide me, sure, but I figured out not to shy away, but to walk towards it all. Live with it, engage, experience. There is nothing to fear."

"Except perhaps the demon who's after me."

"Aye," she said. "There's that. I only had one veil. You have two."

"You see them too," I said, more a statement than a question. "The other veils. The demons."

"Nope," she said. "I'm witch."

"But…"

I pointed at Trebor, who had his massive paws on his groin to keep his cocks at bay.

"Yes, curious, that," Marie said. "But I believe because he's yours, I get to see him."

Mine. I didn't want him. "He's a part of me," I said, more to myself than Marie. "Like Friend."

There they were, my two halves, sitting on either side of Marie.

"That doesn't make you bad, you know," she said.

"But part of me is demon," I said.

"So the fuck what?" she said.

Her profanity made me giggle, and she laughed too. She set her teacup onto the coffee table and gave both Friend and Trebor scratches behind their ears. They snuggled into her plentiful bosom and purred.

"Demons aren't all bad," she said, "nor are witches all good. Same as humans. Good and evil is too simplistic a concept. But I do know this—you weren't concerned about being jailed. Your concern was whether you deserved to be jailed. That speaks volumes."

"If the demon, Empusa, wants me dead, why doesn't she just kill me?"

"Means she doesn't want you dead," Marie said with a shrug. "What I do know about demons is that they rarely give a figgity fuck about the death of humans. They much prefer them alive and suffering."

Trebor's brow furrowed as he glared at Marie.

"So I've heard," she clarified.

"Empusa," I said. "Is she… Did she murder those people?"

"No idea," Marie said. "But it's doubtful. Demons have no real power on this side of their veil. They are but riders. They latch to despicable humans who have atrocious capabilities."

I thought of those horrible creatures, the oversized gnats riding on the shoulders of Bobby and Allison.

"She wasn't riding," I said.

"Not when you saw her," Marie said.

I thought of Empusa, of Kaz's discomfort with her, of how she glared right into me.

"I left her back on the mainland," I said.

"She will find you, I suspect," Marie said.

Death finds me. Always.

"What do I do?" I asked.

"What was your plan?" she asked. "Yours and Liza's?"

Liza. We had just found each other again, and so much more.

"We didn't have one," I said.

"Do you now?"

To live. I hadn't desired that before. Now…

"She thought maybe I needed to reconnect with nature," I said. "My roots."

"Wise one, that woman," Marie said with a twinkle in her eye. "She knows you. And cares. Deeply."

Warmth flushed over my body, and I couldn't help but smile.

"Suppose you should keep moving," Marie said. "You're welcome to stay here, but momentum might take you somewhere."

"I think we need to go back," I said. "To the mainland. I want to speak to Empusa."

"You aren't afraid," Marie said.

"I am strong," I said.

We all smiled—me, Marie, Erinyes, Gus, Trebor, and Friend.

Marie heaved herself off the couch, ruffled both Friend's and Trebor's heads, then walked me to the door. Before placing her hand on the knob, her face scrunched in concern. Maybe concentration. She started mumbling to herself and looking around until she spotted something on a desk by the window that gave her pause.

"Here," she said. "Take this."

She handed me a wine stopper, a different one from the Empusa one. This one had a foursome of goats on it, carved out of obsidian rock with aurora gems for eyes.

"In case you and Liza actually leave an open bottle with wine left in it." Hearty laughter bellowed straight from her belly.

"Sorry we drank all your wine," I said sheepishly.

"I'm quite pleased you did," she said.

With no more words, and a firm hug, Marie sent me out into the night, the goat stopper held tight in my fist.

Chapter Twenty-Five

The farther I moved away from Marie's cottage, the colder it got. The memory of the fire and the warmth of the tea faded, but it sped my steps as I imagined bringing the fire to life in cabin four. How beautiful would those flames be glowing on Liza's golden skin.

I need to get wood.

As if in answer, the trees cracked and swayed. I walked a touch faster, nearly a sprint, but the path was becoming rougher, the trees closer together, and soon I had my arms in front of me, pushing away branches that threatened to gouge out my eyes. I'd slowed considerably to fight my way through the thick brush.

Was it like this when we came?

Of course not.

Many journeys through the woods at Eden's Edge to the cemetery and back were just like this. Impossibly and suddenly dense, dark, and full of shadows.

"Might as well come out and say hello," I said.

No one came. I didn't except they would. Things that

meant to unsettle me rarely did what they were told.

I didn't stop moving. I figured I had to eventually reach cabin four, though I was treading a different path than the one Marie and I had.

Why do I ever go into the woods?

BECAUSE YOU LOVE IT, Trebor said. DIRT WITCH.

Being with Marie and remembering my feet in the earth—Mom, Miss Mojo, Gus, gardens, birds, and life—made me want to find out more about the dirt in me.

A droplet of moisture hit my face.

I tried to walk faster. Branches whipped at my face, clawed my arms and chest. I didn't slow, though, not until the forest forced me to. A thick tangle of brush and deadfall blocked the path, and I could see no other way. I half debated returning to the cottage and having Marie come back with, but my flight response egged me to move forward. I would have to find a way around.

Another droplet of moisture dripped on my cheek.

I looked up. My dad—The Blankness in moniker, Khuya by name—was there, watching me, his long blank body and face contorted around the trees like a black branch. Erinyes was screeching and flapping, and if she had a beak, she'd likely be pecking at his face. Friend was there, too. Her limbs were branches, all bends and length, and she crouched below my dad, watching something behind me on the path.

Ignoring the commotion above, I turned and found a set of glowing green eyes.

"You can't be here," I said to the coyote. "There are none of you on the island."

But there he was, teeth bared, tail between his legs, and hackles raised.

"Get," I yelled and clapped my hands over my head.

Coyotes were skittish. This little fucker should've run, but he didn't. He took a step forward, slow, stalking. I brayed and waved my arms, trying to make myself as big as I could.

It's not a bear, Khuya whispered in my ear, and his long, forked tongue slipped down my shirt between my breasts.

I grabbed that rancid tongue and ripped it clear from his head. It scorched my palm with its heat, and dark maggots writhed beneath my freshly blistered skin.

Atta girllll, he hissed. *That's Daddy's little devil.*

I shot a glance at the wall of brambles blocking my path and frantically searched for another route.

If you run, he runs, and you can't outrun a beast like that, Khuya said.

"What do I do?" I said, but not to him. Never to him.

You are smart, he said. *You are strong. No man or beast is any match for you.*

The forest silenced, and all my senses honed to the attack. The whoosh of the wind moved to my ears when the coyote jumped through the air. His rotten teeth stank of carrion as his mouth opened wide, positioned to rip out my throat. He was a mere meter from me when my demon arm snapped out and grabbed him by the throat. He mewled and yelped as I grasped his mangy, emaciated body in my hands and twisted, cracking his spine right in the middle. His body went limp, but his mouth kept chomping, and that shrill scream kept bellowing from his throat.

"Are you crying?" I asked the mutt. My voice was low, dark and gritty with glass. "Are you whinging for your mommy, you little bitch?"

Moisture dribbled from his eyes, and blood spurted from his mouth. The sight and smell of it roused something within me. Something hungry and full of rage. I licked the salt of his tears and held his corpse above my head to chug the blood pouring from his body. Once he was bled dry, the horror and shame set in. I lowered his empty, shriveled body to the ground and thrust his leg into my mouth, munching fur and grinding bones between my jaws.

I didn't do that. Couldn't do that, kill like that, and if there was no evidence left behind, no one would ever know. I punched my fist in to its stomach and shoved its entrails into my mouth, gulping and swallowing like a snake until a branch behind me cracked under the weight of a foot.

"Anna?"

No!

"Don't look at me," I said.

My voice warbled. It was once more my own, and my body was small again—pale and weak and shivering.

Liza knelt beside me and wrapped a blanket around my shoulders. "Impressive," she said.

But she didn't sound impressed. She sounded scared.

"It was going to attack me, and I—" My hands were covered in blood, fur, and clumps of wet bone dust. The corpse in front of me was steaming, shredded, the surrounding trees splattered and dripping with gore, black fur, and so much meat...

"No," I said as I opened my hands and let the bowls of the beast roll onto the ground. "It was a coyote. A mangy little fuck, and he lunged at me, and—"

There were no coyotes on the island. Marie reiterated that.

"Come on," Liza said. "You're freezing. I'm freezing. Let's get back to the fire."

"Wood," I said. "I went to get wood."

She let out a small laugh. "Well, I know it's dark, but you really went the wrong way," she said. "Unless you intended to chop the trees yourself. Or rip them with your bare hands, I suppose."

How did she find humour in any of this? Me, the human...

...MONSTER...

...She was traveling with, who just disemboweled and ate a whole-ass animal of some sort, and she wasn't horrified.

She'd seen me like this before. She'd seen my change, seen me murder a human piece of filth that had beat and defiled her.

Friend and Trebor were standing side by side on the trail. It was clear now, and I couldn't help but wonder if they were the ones who cleared it.

Liza helped me to my feet and wrapped me in the woolen blanket. I was naked and barefoot, and wondered where my clothes had gone. Burst off me like they had in that alley? Liza led me down the trail, which had been smoothed to protect my feet. I looked back at Trebor and Friend who were following us, snapping at each other with sharp teeth and swiping talons at each other like petulant siblings.

And beyond them, on the path towards the cottage, was Khuya with Erinyes on his shoulder. They were watching me like loving parents. Or disappointed ones. Or a combination of both.

Chapter Twenty-Six

Liza and I didn't speak of the incident in the woods. She bathed me, cleaning away dirt and the remnants of beast. We found old clothes in one of the dresser drawers. I brushed the meat out of my teeth while Liza got the fire going again.

There would be no more sleep this night. It was almost dawn, regardless. I had been gone all night; by the time we got back to cabin four, it was just over half past four. So, I put on a pot of coffee while Liza stoked the fire to raging.

We sat and warmed our bones on the rug, steaming cups in our hands, leaned up against each other.

"I don't care," Liza said.

"About what?"

"That animal," she said. "Or those dead bodies, or about anything you might have done or might be."

"I'm sorry," I said.

"For what?"

"For taking so long. For…Bobby and Allison. What they did to you before I figured out…"

Liza's eyes glazed over, and she gazed into the fire. I don't know if she realized it, but her knees closed tight together, and her shoulders tensed.

Maybe we would talk one day about her trauma. Maybe we wouldn't. Maybe it was eating her from the inside out. I hoped I could alleviate some of that pain.

"You didn't know," she said. "Not that you didn't know what you were capable of, it's that you didn't know what they were capable of."

Rape. Torture. Murder.

So much depravity in the world. I wished I could sweep the streets every night with my teeth and talons and be rid of it all.

"So, what's the plan?" she asked.

I never told her about my nighttime tea with Marie. She didn't ask where I'd gone and what I had been doing. I supposed that part of me was mine. She couldn't understand.

"I say we drive on," I said.

"To where?"

"Where did you have in mind when we came here?" I asked.

"All I had on my mind was away," she said. "Far away from Vancouver, from those murders. Put the ocean between us and all of that."

"Let's keep going," I said. "North to the Haida Gwaii. Take it one day at a time."

"Sounds good," Liza said. "I'll head to the longhouse and square up with Marie if you gather up our stuff."

"You can try," I said. "I suspect our money is no good here."

We got up from the rug and were about to go about our business, but once we were on our feet, facing each other, time and everything stopped.

"Was it real?" Liza said.

She wasn't talking about the coyote in the woods.

"It was for me," I said.

She kissed me, and I put my hands on the small of her back and pulled her in until our bodies were pressed together. Heat flushed between my legs, and I worked their way up her shirt, cupping her braless breasts.

"No," we said in unison, then laughed.

"We got places to be," I said.

She smiled, licked my lips, and headed out the door towards the longhouse.

We didn't have much to pack. I piled our clothes and bags on a chair and picked up Marie's blanket to fold it up. Something fell out, clattered to the floor, and rolled under the chesterfield. I got on my hands and knees to retrieve whatever had dropped. I couldn't see the dark underbelly of that chesterfield, so I swept my hand under and grabbed the hard, metallic object. I pulled it out and was greeted by four pairs of eyes.

"Right," I said.

I had forgotten the four-headed goat stopper Marie had given me. I was tempted to leave it behind—she'd been generous enough already, and this looked quite expensive. Marie wanted me to have it. Or it had wanted me.

"Ready?" Liza said.

I tucked the goats into my pocket. "That was quick," I said.

"Marie wasn't there. I left some cash under the counter with a note."

I wondered where Marie was. My heart ached a touch. I had known her so briefly, but I already missed her.

The road rumbled a song as we bumped and jiggled our way out of the woods and onto the highway heading north. The paved road wasn't much better. The farther north we travelled, the less travelled the road was. Once we were on the smoother pavement, though, I realized part of the rumbling wasn't the road, but my stomach.

"Can we stop for food?" I asked.

"Next stop is Coombs," Liza said. "Lots of little spots there."

Perfect. I wondered if we could hide on the island forever. Certainly there'd be news reports and bulletins advertising my face. And maybe Liza's. The thought of her being hunted and punished for my crimes—or crimes related to me—made me nauseous. I was so, so happy she'd come back into my life, but I wasn't good for her. I wasn't good for anyone.

I'm not good.

The landscape whizzed by the window as we drove, a stunning collage of trees, water, and dogwood. But I didn't gaze or even steal a glance, no matter how much I wanted to. Because in my peripheral all I could see were pale faces and too-long limbs, wide mouths with sharp teeth, talons, and cocks. Outside the car was hell, pain, and death. Inside the car was peace and love.

Liza, noticing my discomfort, took my hand. A flash of movement from the backseat caught my eye. I expected Friend, Trebor, or Gus and Erinyes squabbling like siblings. But it was none of them.

In the back of the car, strapped into a car seat, was a blank little child—no hair, no face, no belly button, no genitals. Just a small, smooth human swinging their feet in time to the music on the radio.

"That's new," I muttered.

"Are you okay?" Liza asked.

I looked out the windshield, trying not to notice the child behind us. "Sorry, what?" I said.

"I was thinking fast food," she said. "Maybe a drive-thru or something. We could find a nice picnic table somewhere with more nature and fewer people."

"That'd be nice," I said.

The movement in the backseat intensified, as did my anxiety. I looked back again. The child was encased in a caul, frantically trying to rip their way out. They couldn't breathe. I could feel it in my chest, my lungs. I gasped in unison with the child, and they reached for me, stretching the caul, pleading silently—

"What's going on?" Liza asked.

"They can't breathe," I panted.

Liza slowed the car until it rolled to a stop on the shoulder. She killed the engine, let go of my hand, and just watched and listened.

"I… There's…" I stammered. "I know you can't see, but there's a child, and they…"

Liza said nothing. Just watched and listened.

"Okay," I said. "Okay. Okay."

The child was clawing at their throat now, their breathing quick and shallow. Their bowels and bladder released, creating a snow globe of filth in that caul.

My hand shot forward as a talon, slicing through the caul and spilling the contents—piss, shit, child—onto the seat and floor of the car. A pause, a beat, then the explosive wail of a newborn baby filled my ears and skull. I wailed, too, keening and rocking in my seat while Liza held the sides of my head.

Then everything was silent. The backseat was empty, the crying had ceased, and the stench of death had been replaced by the soft aroma of dogwood and ocean.

I stepped out of the car, brushed the ghost filth off my clothes, and breathed deep the air of the island. Liza came out and stood beside me until I'd composed myself, then we got back in the car.

Friend was there now, in the back seat, the child held against her body. Though the child had no face, and no mouth through which to drink, it was guzzling hungrily from Friend's engorged left breast, milky black fluid tricking down Friend's body and the babe's cheek.

I was so tired. So, so tired.

"Can we keep going?" Liza asked.

"Yes please."

So, we drove. We saw only minimal signs of life along the highway—a few cars, some deer, an indie gas station or two. I was almost ready to cave and go for a stale gas station sandwich when my eye caught a business just off the highway—a large market, parking lot full of cars, and a very peculiar roof.

"There," I said.

"There?" Liza asked. She sounded hesitant but hit the brakes and pulled into the parking lot.

"It's busy," she said. "And there's no drive thru."

"I know."

"We'd have to go inside," she said.

"That's okay."

"They might not do takeaway."

"Even if they do," I said, "I'd like to eat here, if it's all right with you."

She nodded. She had to circle the lot a few times to find an empty parking spot. Once she did, I nodded to Friend, who was still breastfeeding in the back seat. She waved me on. So, I left her there with the child. Liza and I stood behind the car, looking at the market with the sod on its roof.

"Cool," she said.

"Yeah," I said.

"I'd heard about this place, but I've never been," she said. "I'm glad we stopped."

"We had to," I said.

In my left, hand I clutched the wine stopper with the carving of the goat heads. *Funny, that.* I stared at the roof of the market, which was covered in sod, and the four goats meandering there, snacking on the grass.

Chapter Twenty-Seven

"Do you think she knew about this place?" Liza asked, "Marie'?"

We were seated on the patio with a great view of the goats meandering around the roof. As soon as the waitress seated us, I showed Liza the bottle stopper. I didn't tell her about my night in that cottage, only that Marie had given me those goats.

"What could she have known?" I asked.

"That we were coming this way. That we would drive by this, and we should stop."

"No," I said. "She would've just told us to pop in here for a coffee or some food. I don't think she really knew what she was suggesting."

I rolled the bottle stopper over in my hand. The aurora eyes with their rectangular pupils glistened at me under the naked bulbs strung around the patio.

"Get you ladies something to eat?" the waiter asked.

Both Liza and I started at his sudden appearance.

"So sorry," he said as he took a step back from the table.

"Not you," I assured him. "We're just a little on edge."

"So maybe no coffee," he said with a smile.

"Oh, no no," Liza said. "All the coffee. Just bring the pot."

We all chuckled, a nervous trio, and he left us with the menus and told us to take our time.

"What do you think it means?" Liza asked. "The goats?"

"No idea," I said. "Maybe there's something here. Or maybe we aren't supposed to go farther than this. I dunno."

"What did you see in the car?"

What I saw was a testament to my sanity. I was different, I wasn't quite human, witch, or demon, but I still attributed everything to my mental health. And for some reason, that was worse.

"A child," I admitted.

"As in a baby?"

"Yeah," I said. "In a car seat."

I didn't tell her about the caul, or about Friend breastfeeding with her sour, grey milk.

"Okay." Liza moved her jaw, looking for the words.

Perhaps she was trying not to react. I wondered, most times, how much she was having to restrain herself from running away screaming.

"Was it a little boy or a girl?" she asked.

"I don't know. They were blank," I said. "No face, genitals, nipples, or bellybutton."

"Oh," Liza said.

"Yeah," I said.

The waiter slinked up to the table.

"Have you decided?" the waiter asked with a much gentler approach.

"Coffee," Liza said.

"What do you recommend?" I asked.

"Are you vegan? Vegetarian?" he asked.

I eat human flesh by the kilogram.

"No, nothing like that," I said. "Unless you consider

bacon a vegetable."

Another tinkle of laughter from the three of us.

"That sounds great," Liza said. "Maybe just some bacon, eggs, and toast."

"Turkey bacon okay?" he asked.

"Do you have real bacon?" I asked.

"Unfortunately, no. Couldn't sell it much after…the island's pork market really took a beating. We'd order less and less, but it was still rotting in storage. We decided, for the few people who still ordered it—tourists mostly—that it wasn't worth the loss."

I turned the goat stopper over in my hand. "What happened?" I asked.

"Oh," he said. "You seemed like you were from around here."

"We…" Liza bit her lip. Her eyes grew wide and panicked—a deer ready to flee.

"Mainlanders," I said. "But we came here plenty as children."

"It was on the mainland, a long time ago," he said. "That whole mess was, what, decades ago, I think?"

Decades. Back when we were just escaping Eden. A cold chill rippled through my body, and panic sweat started to bead on my skin.

"What mess?" I asked, though it came out a barely a breath.

The waiter checked to see if anyone was listening, then leaned over our table. He was telling us a secret or a disturbing truth not meant for other ears.

"You ever hear about the Pickton Farm?"

My stomach dropped. Liza's jaw clenched.

"Guessing you have," he said. "What do you know?"

"He was a bad man," Liza said.

"Understatement," the waiter mumbled.

I gave him a look.

He understood. "Well… You can read up on him if you like, but the whole thing soured people on pork for the longest time."

Bobby was a bad man. He trafficked, raped, murdered. I wanted to ask about the pork, but Liza was squirming in her seat. I hadn't suffered like she had at the hands of that bastard.

"I don't really know all that much about it," I said. "I know he died. And that he'd… Was he from the island here?"

"Mainland," the waiter said. "Inland. The farm was near Port Coquitlam."

Halfway between here and Eden's Edge.

"That farm supplied the western half of the province with pork. Big production. After it shut down, pork sales waned, but not just because of supply. People didn't want it."

"I was very young," I said. "When he died. And I…I didn't watch the news."

No news in the foster homes. By the time I was on my own, on the streets, there was no news there, either. And I'd made zero attempts at searching up anything around the timeframe of the razing of Eden's Edge.

"I need to use the restroom," Liza said.

She'd done so when we first arrived. The expression she gave me when she got up from the table told me she wasn't leaving to pee. Once she was gone, through the busy restaurant and into the bathrooms at the back, I looked into the waiter's wide eyes. He wanted to tell someone so bad. So many true crime junkies.

"Bobby was a serial killer, you know," he said.

"I know that much," I admitted.

"Did you know about the farm?"

I shook my head.

"Bobby drove trucks up and down the coast, sometimes into the central mainland. Had a penchant for picking up strays, if you know what I mean."

Oh I know. I thought of Mary, of her limp body as he

drove away that last night in Eden.

"RCMP found oodles of evidence on that farm," the waiter whispered. "Rumour has it, they found his truck and his burnt-out body in some commune in the Okanagan. Once they identified him, dental records and whatnot, they visited the farm. Quite the find."

"Did they find…"

People? Women? Children?

"Bodies," he said. "And a torture trailer full of toys and shackles, that whole mess. But that's not the worst part."

Never is.

"They excavated and tested the land. The livestock. He fed the used-up bodies to his pigs."

I could tell by the look on this poor boy's face that he wanted me to be shocked. That he thought I should be. But I, too, had consumed full bodies, bones and all. The pig that I am.

"Awful," I said, because I should. "How many?"

"Pigs?"

"Bodies."

"They never said. Topped a hundred, though. Not sure they could get an accurate count. Dude'd been fucking around since the 90s, so god knows how many people and pigs he went through."

And how much human flesh the populous of western Canada had eaten.

"Yuck," I said.

"Indeed," he said.

"And the farm is closed now, I assume."

"And heavily guarded. Pickton had family that tried to come by, but they were no-good terrors as well. The whole place was condemned and locked down. Trying to keep the tourists out too, I suppose."

"Who would want to visit that?" I asked.

I wanted to do that. To see his victims—many of them

who I could've saved by acting sooner than I did. I was so self-involved trying to conjure the witch side of myself that I neglected what the demons were showing me.

"Oh plenty," he said. "True crime junkies, all that."

"I suppose."

Liza came out of the bathroom. There was little colour in her normally golden face. She paused, making eye contact with me to tell me she was coming and could we shut the conversation down please.

"Thank you," I said to the waiter and nodded towards Liza.

He took the hint, then walked the other way to avoid her as she returned to the table.

"Any new info?" she asked.

"Plenty," I said. "Not sure if it's useful, though."

She hugged herself. Somehow, on that short trip to and from the restroom, her hair had grown a tad straggly, her cheeks a bit more sunken.

"Trauma," I said. "You suffered a great deal."

"You too," she said.

"Not like you."

Nothing like you.

"I'm okay," she said.

"You're not. But you don't have to be. I'll be with you until you are, or if you never are. I'll just be here, and you can just…be."

Her smile crinkled the corners of her eyes, and tears leaked out. The dam had been broken, and she hid her face in her napkin to hide her sobbing. No one would have noticed if it wasn't for the high-pitched wailing.

"I'm here," I said.

I walked to her side of the table, pulled a chair up beside her, and put my arm around her heaving shoulders. I was going to bark at the looky-loos to mind their business, but when I looked around the restaurant, I found that no one was noticing Liza's loud sorrow.

Another ear-piercing sob, but not a single head turned.

The sound wasn't coming from Liza.

She was crying, her body trembling, but only soft trembles of air were blowing out of her mouth. The mewling, loud and ringing, originated from somewhere outside of the market.

My body tensed. I wanted to go, to help, but I realized the sound was only for me. I was the only one who could hear it, and Liza needed me.

"Go," she said. "Go?" She sat up and touched my face. "Something's happening," she said. "Do you see anything? Hear voices? Smell?"

I nodded.

"I'll be fine," she said. "I'm going to sit here and drink more coffee than I should. It's rotting my body but making me happy."

I didn't budge.

"Hey," she said, forcing a smile. "Could be worse. I could be snorting eight balls and downing a two-four every night."

True. But that didn't mean things were okay. Just because there were worse things didn't mean her bad was any less painful or valid. It was hers, and it was awful, and we'd face it together.

But I had to find the source of that incessant racket before my eardrums burst. I kissed her on the forehead as I left the table. She poured another cup of coffee as I walked away.

I followed the sound through the cafe, the bustling market inside, and out the back door to a park, and green space beyond. The sound didn't get any louder as I got closer, but the air shifted, like an increase in pressure. All other noises got muffled, then quiet, then silent as I reached a little playground tucked back against the edge of the woods. There was a swing set there, one swing swaying in the breeze, back and forth. Except there was no breeze, and the other swing was still.

I sat on the moving seat and pumped my feet, flying higher and higher until my hair became wings, lifting me to the sky. I smiled and laughed, my mouth opened wide. The stench hit me like a wall. I gagged, choked, and dragged my feet in the dirt to bring the swing to a stop. The air was dense with the stench of moisture, manure, and blood. And rummaging around the playground was a drove of pigs. Their faces and hooves were slick with the sheen of blood and fat. No wonder since their snouts were buried eyeball deep in bodies strewn about the playground.

I jumped off the swing and walked slowly, taking care to avoid stepping in any piles of death or pig shit as I weaved my way back to the market and cafe. I didn't recognise any of the bodies as I passed, but there was a certain familiarity. The pigs were in the process of devouring all the torsos and what lay beneath, but that's not where they'd started. All the eyes on all the people had been chewed out, leaving hollowed, ragged sockets in their place.

Impossible for a pig to do.

But it was impossible for these pigs and bodies to be here at all. They weren't here. The veil was blowing in the breeze of my mind, revealing something I should see.

I knew where we had to go.

"Everything okay?" Liza asked when I returned to the table. "I mean, no, but..."

"No imminent danger," I said.

It was the best I could do most days. And I was never very sure of that, either.

The waiter returned.

"If you want to get anything from the market on your way out, you can pay your bill at the till with your other stuff. Let me grab you the tab."

"We're heading out?" Liza said as the waiter disappeared.

"Yeah," I said. "And let's do that—hit the market on our

way out. Some food and beverages for the road. We have a long drive and another ferry ride ahead of us."

Chapter Twenty-Eight

Marie was right. There was a ferry terminal in Nanaimo that was so close and would have saved us some driving if we weren't trying to throw off any pursuers. This time, we took the car with us on the ferry. They wouldn't be searching for this car, so Liza didn't mind boarding with it. She seemed awfully prepared for a getaway, and it made me wonder, not for the first time, what had happened during her youth. Did she live on the streets like me? Did she stay in foster care, or with a loving family who saw her to adulthood? She didn't mention a family, and she was very much alone now, so I figured her past was as blotchy and dark as mine.

I hoped I'd have enough time with her to find out all about it.

She tried to get me to rest in a cabin for the trip, but I wanted to stay outside. I was pretty sure I'd see all sorts of horrible things chasing us, in the water behind us and in front of us, but I'd hidden inside for long enough. I wanted the sea air, the salt, the smell of thick forests waiting for us on either side.

She got us more coffee, like she had before, and some steaming poutine, which I picked at because I knew I needed to eat. I looked up from my food and over the water once or twice. It was the same as what it had been on the journey to the island—blue sky and sunny life behind us as we barreled towards death and fire.

It's me. Not the land itself. Wherever I'm headed, death awaits.

I wondered if I headed for space if the stars and planets would light aflame and die horrible, screaming deaths.

The boat rocked us into tranquility, and we leaned against each other, her head on my chest and my face in her hair. By the time we reached the mainland, we were nodding off. The announcements over the speakers jarred us to attention, and we hustled down to our vehicle.

"I wish I could drive," I said. "Give you a break."

"I like driving," Liza said. "It liberating. Like I'm getting away."

As she jangled the keys in her hands, she studied them, looking for words. Or knowing the words but deciding whether she should speak them aloud. Audible words make a thing more real.

"I ran so far, Anna. That night. So far, and I was nearly naked, frozen, and my feet were bleeding. They're so ugly now. Gnarled and scarred, all my toenails are off."

She laughed. "Like bird's feet," she said.

Erinyes landed on her shoulder and ruffled Liza's raven black tresses with a scarlet wing.

"I wish I'd had a car then," she said. "So, I learned to drive as soon as I could. And I drive every day. Even if I'm not going anywhere. Just kilometer after kilometer, distance behind me and freedom ahead."

She opened the door, got in, and reached over to unlock mine. I'd never had a car. I'd never driven. I didn't feel the need for constant motion like she did, but at least, she didn't have her head buried in the sand.

OR A SQUIRREL UP HER PUSSY.

"Fuck off."

Liza's eyes moistened in pity. "That wasn't for me," she said.

"No," I said. "It's him. Trebor."

"Trebor?"

I hadn't talked to her about him. And not much about Friend. One day, I hoped to explain it all, to her and myself.

"He's me," I said. "Like Friend. The two halves."

"Ah," she said, though I'm not sure she understood or believed.

I didn't, either.

It was only about an hour's drive from the ferry terminal at Horseshoe Bay to Port Coquitlam. We could've done it in less, but we opted to avoid Vancouver all together. We hadn't seen any news, but I figured there would be a manhunt, and Vancouver proper would be swarming with people who'd seen our pictures. They had little to go on. I had no connections and a blank slate of a past. I hoped Liza was the same, but regardless, we'd left no obvious trail and avoided any heavily populated areas.

The long route took us north of the city, along the edge of Pinecone Burke Provincial Park and back down to Port Coquitlam. We stopped at a grungy, no-name gas station on the outskirts of town. While Liza pumped the gas— something else I'd never done, I wandered inside to look around; not much except snacks, drinks, and roadside kitsch like air fresheners, post cards, and lighters shaped like a woman's bare breasts and torso.

"Whatcha need?" the clerk asked with an Irish lilt. She was young with green hair, dark brown eyes, and a swath of freckles across her button nose.

I picked up the lewd lighter and cocked a brow.

"Yeah," she said. "Not from around here, are ye?"

"Not far," I admitted.

She was safe. I knew it in my bones. And even if she wasn't, we were probably reaching the end of the line, anyhow. The doom ached in my bones.

"Round here," she said, "folks like that kind of shit."

I flipped the lighter over in my hand, studying the painted mound of hair at the apex of the thighs, and the too-dark, too-pointy nipples in the center of perfectly round breasts.

"It's awful," I said, and tossed it on the counter. "I'll take it."

Greenhair chimed her laughter

"Alice," I read her name tag aloud.

"Not of Wonderland," she said with a grimace as she motioned around the grubby shop.

"Kyteler," I said.

"What's that now?" she asked.

Liza came in, saw us chatting, and took her time coming up to the counter.

"Alice Kyteler," I said. "First woman accused of witchcraft in Ireland. It was the early 1300s or so. Four husbands, all of them dead. They accused her of all sorts of things."

Alice's eyes were wide, and her mouth curved into a smile.

"Cool," she said. "Was she executed?"

"No," I said. "She fled. Disappeared."

"Ooooh," Alice cooed. "Perhaps I am that damsel after all."

"Alice," I said. "The pig farm."

Her smile faded.

Liza grabbed my arm, startling me. "Don't," she whisper-scolded me.

I didn't listen.

"What about it?" Alice asked.

"It's around here?" I asked.

"Uh huh," she said, then bit her lower lip. "What do you want with that place?"

"Anyone go there?" I asked.

"Not for years," she said. "Decades, maybe. They got it locked-up tight."

Her eyes flickered upwards. It was slight, but I caught it. I, too, looked to the ceiling. Friend was stuck in the corner, straddling the security camera. She draped her hair over it, then did it again in a purposeful motion.

I laughed, startling Liza and Alice. "True crime junkies," I said, pointing at Liza then at my chest. "Softies, though. I hate actually going to the places. Just wanna do a drive-by, you know?" I winked, so slightly that it evaded the path of the camera.

"Well, I wouldn't recommend that. But I do know of some cool ghost hunting spots in the area. I'll write the addresses."

"I can just put the address in my phone," Liza offered.

"Nah," Alice said. "Maps'll take you to the wrong places. Always does, every app. I'll write out the directions." She scratched a pen on that pad for over a minute. "Here ye go."

I slid by a confused Liza and took the folded piece of paper from Alice. "Thanks," I said.

She winked.

"What was all that?" Liza asked. "And you better be careful, yapping to strangers like that. We're liable to get caught sooner than later."

I cringed. I didn't care if I was caught, but I didn't want anything to happen to her. "You're right," I said. "I'm sorry."

I got in the car, and Liza started the engine. I unfolded the paper and read the first line, which was underlined five or six times for emphasis.

Go left out of the parking lot. It's the wrong way, but I don't want you to go the right way, or someone will know I spilled the juice.

"Go left," I said to Liza

She didn't ask any questions. Not yet.

Drive through the four-way, then two sets of lights, and take a left at the next four-way. Then left again on Carsten Street. From there, you'll head to Highway 40 where you'll turn right. Keep going until you reach Faulten Lane on your left. Another 4 kliks or so, and the farm will be on your right. Look for the faded sign with the pigs on a palace. Go to the red bench and park in the ditch. The grass will hide you.

I gave Liza all the directions, one at a time. It brought us to the highway, a busy two-lane road, then to Faulten Lane, which was a narrow gravel road pitted with potholes and ponds of rainwater. I knew the farm when we reached it. There'd only been a few properties, and they were spaced out with great green spaces and tree borders between. This farm was particularly large and overgrown with weeds, vines, and branches that snaked over the structures and rusted-out vehicles abandoned in the yard.

"Here," I said, but Liza was already slowing.

"No, don't stop," I said. "Keep driving up to the red bench in the ditch. It's about five-hundred meters up the road."

That's what the note told me. We saw the red bench at the same time, and I motioned for her to pull onto the shoulder.

"In the ditch," I said. "It'll hold. Just so we're in the tall grass."

"What?"

I flashed the note at her. She scanned the page. Her mouth shriveled into a tight line. She wasn't very happy with this. Regardless, she did what the note said and pulled into the ditch.

"Now what?" she asked.

"Now we walk."

Chapter Twenty-Nine

It had been a long day, and I didn't envision it ending anytime soon. It was early evening when we trudged through the woods, giving the Pickton Farm a wide berth to approach it from behind. Alice's note said there'd be a purple-and-silver scarf tied to the bottom picket of the back fence. The board there could be removed, and the chicken wire lining the fence would be cut.

"Guess people frequent this place after all," Liza said.

Of course they did. People were obsessed with death and depravity. Even being in its orbit was a thrill

The silver thread in the scarf caught our torch beam right away. Liza lifted away the board. I crawled through. I was always going to go first. I didn't want her hurt, and I wasn't sure that I could get hurt. I didn't wish to find out, but I'd rather it be me than her.

The first building on the farm, a long barn, was a ways away. The field felt so exposed, so I started moving along the perimeter of the fence, aiming my torch just past my feet rather than straight ahead. After walking to the end of the fence and changing direction towards the road and the front of the farm, I noticed Liza's torch beam was no longer at my heels.

"Liza?"

There was nothing behind me. No light, no Liza, only the total black of a starless night.

"Liza," I said, louder and firmer than before.

The only response I got was muffled breathing.

"Liza, are you hurt?"

I jogged back the way I'd come, taking care to watch my feet so I didn't step on her if she'd collapsed. Good thing I did, because I found her sitting on the ground, arms wrapped around her knees, rocking. I knelt beside her and put my hand on her back. Her heart was pounding through her spine.

"Can't," she said.

"Can't what?"

She was shuddering. I held her, and she whimpered. Her face was soaked with tears. Her gaze was fixed on the barn.

"Oh," I said.

Shhe was broken. The pain was still there, the trauma of what Bobby and Allison did to her was fresh. Always would be.

"I'll go," I said. "Let me walk you back to the car."

She shook her head, and that beautiful black-glass mane rippled blue in the night. "I can't go. I can't. I thought I could just power through, but…I don't have to go back to the car. I'll sit right here."

"Liza," I said. "It's dangerous."

She laughed. "Everything is, but I'm less worried about bugs and snakes than whatever might be waiting up there."

I still didn't want her getting bitten. By anything.

"Keep your flashlight on," I said. "I want to be able to turn and see it at all times."

"Yeah," she said. "And I can't quit fucking shaking. It'll be like a disco back here."

I kissed her forehead and held her for a moment before getting up and making a beeline straight for the barn. Fuck stealth. Liza was safe where she was, and I was through pussyfooting around. I wanted to get there, have a look around, and get back to Liza as quickly as possible.

My anxiety stayed steady the entire journey to the buildings. It was there, like a dull hum in my mind, but it wasn't getting any worse. There were eyes on me from the perimeter of the farm. Riders perched like gargoyles sat on the fenceposts, their eyes glowing green in the night.

Are bad people here still? Or is this just remnants of what resided here before?

Decades was a long time for riders to stick around, though I didn't quite understand the science behind the creatures that piggybacked on regular folks like a tainted conscience.

I approached the long barn and slowed my steps. I wasn't convinced this property was empty. There were no lights on, no sound, no movement, but the way Alice had known so much about it made me think this what a spot frequented by partiers, horny teenagers, or worse. I also wondered about security. Were there cameras? Were the cops still watching this place? I glanced back over the field, to the spot where Liza was waiting for me. Sure enough, there was a faint beam of yellow across the sheen of the grass. I waved my light low, and she bounced her beam in return.

She's good. For now.

A broken padlock hung from the door of the barn. Not a good sign, but also not a surprising one. The door didn't scream when I opened it, which meant that someone had been oiling it. A metal door on a property uninhabited for this length of time should have something to say when used, but it stayed silent.

The inside was dark, but it didn't smell awful. That was a good sign; no rotting meat had been here recently, and no livestock. The barn wasn't empty, but there wasn't much sign of life. Mostly it was scattered pieces of equipment, old stalls piled with stale hay, and a myriad cobwebs coating the high corners. Friend was there, tangled in a particularly dense mingle of cobwebs, the white silk streaking through her hair like age.

What will you look like as an old woman?

"You see anything?" I asked her.

My voice started even myself; it was a booming echo in that vast, empty space. Friend skittered high into her corner, hiding, as a rustling erupted from one of the stalls. The hairs on my arms bristled, my hearing honed, and I started sniffing the air.

Faint undertones of hogs and shit. And blood.

I closed my eyes and focused on my body. Used the emotions tamped way down deep inside, the anger and sorrow, summoning them to the surface, visualizing them stretching and splintering bones to make way for new bones, flesh, and muscles. When I opened my eyes, I was pointing at the end stall, but my finger wasn't slender and pale, but long, thick, and black. It tapered off at the wrist, fading into my normal arm and typical body.

"Who's there?" I asked.

The only answer was more shuffling and shifting of hay.

With my weapon of a hand leading the way, I stomped, ensuring my steps were loud enough to announce my arrival in case it was a junkie I didn't wish to startle.

It wasn't a junkie. It was a small woman, dark hair cascading over her body like Liza's. She was young, barely adult if even, and her naked body was bruised, battered, and torn.

I tucked my monster hand behind my back. "Honey. Are you okay?"

The girl opened her mouth, but all that came out was the grunt of a hog.

"Oh."

The girl was already dead. Long ago. Probably two decades ago, if not more.

They all were. The barn was teeming with life. Correction. It had been teeming with life—or rather, death—but the veil had been draped over the stalls, tools, and wall. Now that I chose to see it, I could. A dozen or more women, some still shackled to their stalls, others crawling around on hands and knees, snorting through hay like pigs after truffles. They were all covered in their own filth—shit, menstrual blood, and urine caked in streaks down the insides of their thighs and on their emaciated backsides.

I backed away from the stall with the Indigenous girl inside and nearly tripped over two more who were writhing on the floor, covered in layers of vomit and semen. They were everywhere—girls and women, raped, beaten, starved, and carved, speaking in grunts, squeals, and chuffs.

I was suffocating. Their pain, stench, and noises were drowning me. I burst out of the barn to the back field. The sight of Liza's light sweeping back and forth on the grass calmed me.

"She's okay," I said. My new mantra. "She's okay."

But they were not. The field was no longer a sea of grass but a mass grave, bodies piled four high over every inch of soil, flesh chopped and ground into shining meat that still had a rhythmic beat. The entire field pulsed, all those women's dead hearts beating as one. And on the top of the flesh field, hogs gulped hungrily at the meat, gobbling and shitting it out at the same, constant pace.

How many? How many did you kill, Bobby?

I'm sure there were numbers somewhere—on the internet, on the news. But I bet the law didn't even know an exact number. How could they calculate the many women fed to those animals? Or buried beneath this farm, or ground to dust? They couldn't. But I could see them all now, writhing and struggling, a slurry of living-dead flesh.

I walked away from the field, around the side of the barn, and to the one-story farmhouse near the front of the property. These doors were locked, but I didn't give a good goddamn fuck. I used my taloned fist to rip the door off its hinges and toss it into the yard.

The first room beyond the backdoor was the kitchen. Nothing to see there but bowls of rotten, decayed food that had lost its stench years ago. One side of the hallway led to the living room. Nothing remarkable there either, but I did note a newer pizza box splayed open on the coffee table. The grease on the cheese still had a shimmer. I swiped a finger over it and licked the taste. Not spoiled. Recent.

I didn't call out, though the element of surprise was destroyed when I ripped off that door. I reached the bathroom first; I knew from the stench before I even rounded the corner. I pulled my shirt over my nose and mouth as I entered. The chipped tub was full of needles, empty baggies, and ash. There was a large tobacco can full of used condoms beside the toilet, which was filled with black, runny shit and frothy yellow vomit.

I turned to leave and caught my reflection in the mirror. It was me, but my skin had decayed, my teeth exposed along the sides of my face where my cheeks had rotted off. My hair was long, black, and stringy, draped in tendrils over my bare breasts and protruding ribs.

Friend.

I touched my face, and it felt like mine, all warmth and smooth flesh. But in the mirror, she stood, cupping her face, her necrotic fingers poking through her lack of cheek and scraping against the rotted posts that had at one time been molars.

I left the bathroom and shut the door, hoping to close the stench and vision inside.

The next rooms were bedrooms. It was a large trailer, double wide, with four bedrooms at the back. Practically a palace. In the first room, there was nothing but a stained, thin mattress tossed in the middle of the floor and a British Columbia flag strung over the window. The next bedroom was the same, but the curtain was a towel, and there was the addition of a tilted dresser on three legs. I opened the door to the third room and found movement. A couple of teenagers were splayed on the mattress, a girl on her back on a sleeping pad and a boy grinding on top of her, balls deep.

"Hey," I said.

"Wait your turn," the girl slurred.

"You shouldn't be here," I said.

"You should?" the girl said.

They weren't ghosts but real live teenagers, and they were high. Two more were in the corner, passed out with dried vomit caked down their shirts.

I shut the door.

The final room was the master bedroom. I listened to the birdsong within. A faint blue light shone from beneath that door, spilling onto my pale, bare feet.

But I hadn't taken my shoes off.

I was naked, too, the blue light crawling up my legs, filling every nook, cranny, and orifice. I put my hand on the knob and passed through, my feet sinking into the spongy forest floor.

Chapter Thirty

I was back at Eden's Edge, my feet treading the dirt path again. Nothing remained. All the houses were gone, replaced by pits of ash where basements once were. The steeple of the Beast didn't loom, nor did the wretched home where Allison and her transient boyfriend, Bobby Pickton, had run a trafficking operation with a side of rape and torture. Only two houses remained: the one Mom and I had occupied, and the house built on the foundation of feet—New Friend's house.

Friend was waiting there for me on her front porch, and she wasn't alone. Trebor was there with her, each of them perched on their haunches on the pillars at the top of the front steps, both holding a bowl in their hands. I went to them. They didn't react. They were stone carvings of themselves, and the bowls were filled with fluid. I held my hair back and drank from hers.

Warm and gritty. Blood.

I drank from his.

Cool and salty. Tears.

I looked from bowl to bowl, then face to face, witch to demon. I started cupping blood in my hand and transferring it into the tears, then taking the tears and adding them to the blood. I did this with increasing urgency until the liquid in those bowls was a muddy slurry of blood and tears. I tasted both again: lukewarm, gritty, salty.

The hearts in my body pounded, not together, but in harmony.

I left Friend and Trebor grotesques on their pillars and cut across the land to the place Mom and I had so briefly called home. Not even that. A place to stay. But part of my roots grew there, if only just a sprout.

And Mom remains here. Forever.

The bright ring of red feathers still outlined the property. They grew brighter and bolder the closer I got, despite the falling snow. Except it wasn't snow and didn't taste fresh when I poked out my tongue to catch a flake. It was slick and smoky.

Ash.

Eden's Edge was burning around me. My feet sizzled when I stepped through the embers of buildings, the smouldering grass, and the burning hot gravel paths. My flesh bubbled and blistered as tornados of heat swirled my hair, obscuring my face as I walked. The moisture beneath my arms and breasts and between my legs steamed, and a high-pitched whistle filled my ears. I was a kettle. All of Eden was. And we were boiling.

I arrived.

As I stood at the front walkway just outside the perimeter of dead cardinals, the hell storm ceased. The gravel cooled, my skin turned to gooseflesh, and my blisters drained, shrank, and smoothed like they'd never been there in the first place. There was no fire burning, no ash falling from the sky, no songs of the forest.

There was a woman, though, sitting in the middle of our

old property on the throne fashioned from bone and branch that Old Man Merle, my ghost friend from the cemetery, had made me. Her head was tipped forward, a mop of ginger curls covering her face, her hands lazily draped over the arms of the throne. She was wearing a pair of canvas overalls, no shirt underneath, the straps covering nipples on silicone-enhanced breasts. And on her feet was a rubber boot, just one, green and caked in what looked like shit.

I crossed the line of cardinals and went to her. "Who are you?" I asked when I was a few meters from the throne.

She wasn't so beautiful up close. Her arms were striped with scars, some silver and calm, some fresh, red, and angry. Her breasts were cut up, too—jagged lines carved all over her flesh like a crude game of tic-tac-toe. Blood was drooling from a wound on her face I couldn't yet see, and pooling on the crotch of her overalls, mimicking sexual trauma.

"I can see you," I said. "I'm no ordinary girl."

Friend was behind me, cowering, as Trebor stormed the throne and hovered centimeters above the woman. Friend pulled me to leave. Trebor was poised to attack. He bellowed, and the force of his breath blew back the woman's hair, revealing her face.

"Oh," I said.

Should've seen that coming.

She had no eyes. Bloody tears were streaming down her face, wetting her lips into a ruby smile. She allowed her head to loll back, revealing more cuts on her cheeks, forehead, and neck.

"What happened to you?" I asked.

She stood, and the blood on her crotch spread, gushing now, pouring out of her pant legs and puddling beneath her in a crimson lake. Her hands were in fists, and she raised her arms straight out to her sides like the crucifixion. Slowly, one finger at a time, her left hand opened like a blooming flower. And there they were, her eyes in her left hand, bloodshot, with tendrils of tendons hanging off like worms. I took a step closer to see, to look into those eyes, but she thrust her other fist out in front of her, hand down, and nodded at it.

"What?" I whispered.

Friend was cawing like a bird behind me, scolding and screaming and trying to pull me back. Trebor was growling and baring his teeth, his snake cocks striking at the woman's already damaged throat.

She had something for me.

I put an open palm below her fist. She opened her fingers. Whatever she held in her hand fell into mine, and I closed my fingers around it, and—

"Run!"

They were all screaming. All of them—my old friends from Eden's Edge. Old Man Merle, New Friend, Miss Mojo, Mom, Liza, Laz, Gus, Erinyes… They were standing in a row behind the throne, pointing the opposite way, mouths splitting their faces in two as they hollered in unison, a dissonant screech.

RunRunRunRun.

I ran, across the yard, over the perimeter of cardinal feathers, and back to the freestanding door on the edge of the treeline. I burst through, and my feet left the soft squish of grass, landing squarely on the crunchy filth of the carpet in the trailer's master bedroom on the Pickton Farm.

"Run," Liza whisper-yelled. "What is wrong with you? We have to bail!"

The flashlight was in her hand, and she was here, not out in that field, and…

"The police are here," she said, motioning towards the front of the trailer. "We have to run. Now."

She popped the screen out of the master bedroom window, and I only caught a glance at the room before she launched herself out.

"Come on," she yelled from the freedom of the outside.

But I didn't run. I stayed firmly in place, soaking in the artwork on the wall. Lyrics of a song I knew oh so long ago, written it what I knew was blood.

Fog and steam,
gossamer and pitch,
half-breed, tainted, rotten bitch!

Below the prose was the image of three hearts that had sprouted roots and branches, but it had changed once more. The three hearts had been compressed together, their lines overlapping rather than squished together. The roots and branches had connected in a circle, and around that circle were dots. No, not dots. Images.

I moved closer. Trying to see.

"Anna," Liza yelled, no longer a whisper. "Please Anna. Run."

A cardinal, a squirrel. a coyote, and a fourth image I couldn't quite decipher; it had been smudged with what looked like a finger or thumb.

I wasn't even concerned about the body on the floor. The legs and arms had been detached and were set ten centimeters from their former position on the body. I wasn't sure if it was a man or woman. The person's genitals had not only been cut off, their entire groin had been scooped out. Where breasts might have been, the flesh had been removed right to the bone, exposing ribcage. The person had no curves—they had brown spots polka-dotting the inside of their detached arms with creeks of black rot flowing from each. A junkie, young and very dead.

"Anna."

It was no longer Liza's voice.

"Kaz," I said.

He gently took my wrists and placed the steel bracelets on them, the snap a banshee's wail in my brain.

Chapter Thirty-One

I hoped Liza escaped.

It wasn't that I'd given up. I hadn't, not exactly. And it wasn't that I didn't care what happened to me. I did. But I wasn't concerned about the silver cuffs around my wrists, or the cold bonnet of the cop car on which I sat, or Kaz, or the jail cell waiting for me. I wondered if there was a jail in Port Coquitlam. Probably not. Besides, they'd be looking for higher security for someone like me—an escapee, a fugitive.

Little did they know, no prison could ever hold the likes of me.

"Are you cold?" Kaz asked.

Why did he care? "I'm good," I said.

I wasn't. Things were bad. But I wasn't worried. I was more concerned about what I didn't know yet. I had a puzzle to figure out. I was relieved it wasn't me killing these people. I simply couldn't have killed this one. Liza and I were nowhere near Port Coquitlam when that poor soul inside had lost the fight.

"I didn't do this," I said.

"I don't think you did," he said.

I held my hands in front of my face.

"Why the cuffs, then?" I asked.

"I have to," he said. "I think you didn't do this, or any of the others. But procedure… And I don't believe you're safe."

"Okay," I said. "What's the plan?"

He was alone. When he led me through the trailer and out the front door, I expected an entire light show, red and blue flashing lights and rows of Mounties waiting to tackle me if need be. But there were no cop cars at all. No lights, no fanfare, no backup. He'd come on his own.

"I'm not sure," he said.

He was pacing in front of his car, rubbing his hands through his hair. He was a beautiful man, soft and kind. I felt horrible for him being tangled up in this mess.

"You have no backup," I pointed out.

"No," he said. "I don't."

"Why did you come here?" I asked. "How did you know?"

He sat next to me on the car's bonnet and pulled out his phone. He scrolled through some pictures, and before he showed me, I caught something familiar.

"Is that my apartment?" I asked.

He nodded and handed me the phone.

I swiped through the pictures. It *was* my apartment but had been trashed. The curtains and furniture had been slashed, blood was smeared over the walls, everything glass had been shattered. My kitchen drawers were open and splintered, ripped from their hinges and rails. On the bedroom wall, drawn in blood, was a crude child's drawing of a fat pig with curly hair, bloody 'X's' for eyes. And beneath that, the address to where we were now sitting.

"Does anyone else know?" I asked.

"I should say yes," he said. "I should tell you that there's surveillance, or that there are units on the way. But there's not. There likely will be soon, but I think I threw them off the trail. For now."

"Why? Why did you do that?"

"Because I…"

He ran his hands through his hair again. I debated about reaching over and taking his hand like Liza took mine, but it seemed inappropriate. He was already putting his ass on the line for me for some reason. He'd need only a small nudge to say fuck it all and turn me in, throw me behind bars and never look back.

"I know there's something up," he said. "It involves you, but I don't think you're killing people. I don't think you have anything to do with it. I think it's being done *to* you."

"How do you know?" I asked.

"I know," he said. "I don't know how I know, I just do. And Detective Empusa is so hell bent on us crawling up your ass…"

His hands clenched into tight balls, knuckles white, thumbnails nearly splitting the skin on his pointer fingers.

"You don't like her," I said.

"There's something about her."

She's a lesser demon. Goat leg and brass leg. Hungry for blood and souls and can smell what I am.

"Well," I said. "What do we do now?"

"Anna, what do you think is going on?" he asked. He rubbed his brow, frustrated. "I know you're trying to figure it out, too."

"I am," I said. "And I'm still at a loss."

"Why did you come here?" he asked.

"I had a feeling," I said, not wanting to discuss my past.

"You don't want to tell me," he said.

"No," I admitted. "I don't."

"You can talk to me," he said. "You can trust me."

"No," I said. "I won't put you in any sort of position."

"Okay," he said, an easy concession. "Who else would know you're here? That might do that to your apartment and leave that clue?"

"No one," I said.

Liza had been with me. And she would never.

"Liza?" he asked.

"No," Liza said, coming around the corner of the long barn and shuffling her feet to the car. "I've been with her for days. Since she…got out of the jail."

"Liza," I shouted. I hopped off the police car, took a step towards her, but stopped and turned to Kaz, cocking a brow to ask permission. He nodded.

I ran to her and kissed her. She'd been crying; her tears had streaked through the dirt on her cheeks.

"You should have gone," I told her as I kissed her lips, face, and hair.

"I won't leave you," she said. "Not again."

I wanted to walk her back to the hole in the fence, duck through, return to the car, and drive away. But where would we drive? And would Kaz allow us to go? I suppose if he was going to let us leave, we could simply stroll out the front of the property through the gate that he'd opened.

I studied the gate, the loose padlock hanging from a rusted chain creaking in the breeze.

Cold tingled over my flesh.

"How did you get in here?" I asked him.

"What?" he asked, following my line of sight. "Through the gate. How did you get in here?"

"Through a hole in the fence," I said as I hooked my thumb over my shoulder, motioning to the back of the field. "Because we were trying to sneak, but also because the gate was locked."

He looked at the lock, open and swaying.

"You had a key?" Liza asked.

The minute she asked that, after I'd mentioned it was

locked, he jumped to his feet and drew his weapon.

"Down," he said, firm and quiet. "Alongside the barn. Go until we're in the dark."

We moved without question, following the building until we plunged into the shadow behind. From there, he motioned for us to keep going, and we did until we reached a derelict bailer near the middle of the field.

"Stay here," he whispered. "Out of sight."

We did, but we peeked around the machine while he crouched and hustled back to the barn. Once he reached the light, he stood to full height and brandished his weapon in front of him.

"Hello," he called. "Vancouver PD! Show yourself!"

His steps were determined, and his eyes wide. I imagined him listening for every sound, his vision flickering to every bit of movement. A cluster of millers flapped around a floodlight, briefly drawing his attention, but he quickly glanced back to his path and beyond.

A thing like me would have made an excellent cop. I heard and saw everything, smelled every stench. Like now, on a farm that had long since been devoid of animals, the ripe stank of livestock was thick in the air.

"Empusa," I whispered.

Sure enough, as Kaz moved in front of the barn, his weapon leading the way, she skulked from behind his car. Even from our distance, I could hear the clank-thud-clank of her brass leg and her goat leg carrying her along.

"Where are your girlfriends?" she asked.

"Hands where I can see them," he shouted.

It struck me that a man of his composure, size, and experience sounded like a petrified mouse in the presence of this woman.

"Why are you pointing your weapon at me?" she asked, her hands to the side, empty palms to the sky.

She needs no weapons. Those hands are dangerous

enough.

"Stop," he said. "We can talk."

"We could have talked," she said. "But you chose not to. You chose to go to that harpy's apartment, which was crawling with evidence of her wickedness, and declare it all clear. We were stupid not to verify the truth of your lies. But I caught on real quick, Kaziel. Real quick."

"What's your deal?" he asked. "Why are so hell bent on fucking over this woman?"

"I'm not hell bent on fucking anyone," she said. "Your precious little angel broke the motherfucking law. We are officers of those laws she broke, Kaz."

Her voice was elevated, in tone and urgency, but absent was the sound of a pounding heart.

Cool as a cucumber, little demon.

And he had no idea what he was dealing with.

"Kaz," I said.

Liza grabbed my arm as I bolted towards the barn.

"Kaz!" I called as Empusa stepped closer to him.

He took a step back.

They both heard me, but he was the only one who turned his head. And that gave her the opportunity to strike. With long, brass fingernails, nails that I was quite certain hadn't been there moments before, she swiped at his throat. Though he was looking at me, he must have seen her in his peripheral. He dodged her nails, but not quite in time. Blood sprayed into the air and splattered onto the side of the barn.

I didn't slow, and Empusa didn't back down. He crumpled to the ground before I reached him. I knelt beside him and cradled his head in my lap.

"So sad," Empusa said. "Your boyfriend is dead meat. But then, you like dead meat, don't you?"

Kaz wasn't dead. His cheek and jaw had been shredded by her nails, but she'd missed his neck. I put my hand over Kaz's mouth and looked deep into his eyes, willing him to be still and quiet as blood pooled beneath his head.

"I do love dead meat," I said. "Live meat is too difficult to eat."

"Ha," she said. "Sassy. I like it."

"Don't," I said. "It doesn't like you." I wasn't interested in this woman-thing, or whatever she had planned. "Kaz," I said. "Hold on. I'll get you out of here."

Blood bubbled from his lips as air escaped in a constrained wheeze like air through a straw.

"And just how are you going to do that?" she said. "You think I'm going to let you march out of here?"

"Like I marched out of that jail?" I asked.

"Yeah," she said. "Like that."

"Don't suppose you are," I said.

In my peripheral, I saw Liza crouching at the side of the barn. I didn't turn my head in her direction but moved my eyes her way. She took the hint. She backed away, staying low, moving slow so she wouldn't be detected.

"When I stomp," I said.

"What?" Empusa said.

"Fuck off."

I wasn't speaking to her. I'd been speaking to Liza, and I hoped she heard.

Kaz was still gurgling when I rested his head on the gravel and stood tall. I focused on my hands and torso, picturing my dad's heart in that jar of gin, but envisioned it still beating. His heart was beating in my chest, and all of a sudden, his heart had teeth, eating my heart and my mom's heart in bloody crunches. With each bite, my outer flesh tore, revealing black bone and muscle, longer and stronger than anything I'd ever had. Piercing pain rippled up my back where leathery feathers sprouted, spreading to a full span and cloaking Kaz in my shadow.

"My, oh my, oh my," Empusa said. "We're doing this, I guess."

She changed, too. Her hands sloughed off, revealing spikes for arms like a praying mantis. Her growth, though not substantial like mine, was enough to tear her clothes, which fluttered to the ground like crepe paper. Beneath her Mountie uniform was the body of a beast—a womanly body made of curves and beauty, but covered in fur, all except one leg made of gleaming brass.

She cocked her head, I cocked mine. She was ready to strike and skewer me with those mantis arms when I knelt again.

"Smart to concede, stupid girl."

I am strong.

I am me.

I am a demon and witch.

I pierced my hands through the dirt, soaking its moisture into my skin. The strong taste of manure and soil filled my mouth and lungs, but my breathing wasn't hindered.

Empusa's was, though.

She was prepared for Dad. For the demon side in me. She knew what she was up against because she, herself, was a demon. But she was unprepared for what else I was. Dirt witch, daughter of a witch, commander of the soil.

I'm not sure how I knew it would work, but it did. I thought of Miss Mojo and all the bugs she commanded. I pictured the bees flying from her mouth as I conjured dirt to fill mine. And once I was full, my skin stretched by the compacted soiling running through every vein, I screamed. It was a noiseless bellow, but dirt passed between me and Empusa, then it was filling her.

Until Liza, no one had ever brought me to climax. And this wasn't powerful like that, but it sure was close. Dirt blasted from my body, reconstituting in Empusa's, and my body shivered with pleasure both mental and physical. Her face went from smug and violent to terrified and pained as dirt vomited from her mouth and nose and streamed out of her eyes like muddy tears. She shat dirt, too, a slurry of blackish brown gushing down her legs, tarnishing the brass and clumping in the fur.

By the time I was empty, Empusa was bent over, hands on her knees, dirt, mud, and muck exploding from every orifice. I was most interested in the fact that her eyes, ears, mouth, and nose were obstructed by streams of bloody mud.

I lifted my leg and stomped the earth, quaking the entire Pickton Farm.

I focused on my dad and on my current form as I yanked my hands out of the dirt, wrapped them around Kaz, and flung him over my shoulder like a rag doll.

Liza was already at my side. She had been waiting for that stomp.

We ran to Kaz's car. I not only had no problem being quick beneath his weight, I was able to fish his keys out of his pocket as we moved. He was but the weight of a flea hitching a ride on my shoulder. Key in hole, door open, Kaz and I in the back.

"Drive," I said, and Liza did.

She avoided looking in the rear-view mirror. I had to squeeze to get in the car, and my back was pressed against the roof as I hunched over Kaz for us to both fit. I breathed deep, imagining the salty air of the ocean, the crimson feathers of Erinyes, and the coarse fur of Gus. Crinkling and wrinkling, my skin shrank, fitting itself once again to my bones, which had creaked and contorted their way back to human size. Kaz's head had flopped onto my shoulder, so I held it in place over bumps and potholes as Liza careened down the highway.

"Will it catch us?" she asked.

I imagined she was referring to Empusa. And I wondered if she also thought of me as an 'it'.

"Just keep going," I said. "I'll take care of her if she does."

I was naked. My clothes had split off me back at that farm,

which presented an entirely new problem. Empusa knew about me, but she was a demon and didn't matter much. Not in the traditional-world sense. But my clothes were evidence, and they'd been left behind at yet another crime scene. I didn't know how I'd explain all of this away.

Kaz murmured, and I ran my hand through his hair, just like he did when he was stressed.

"I got this," I said to him. "I'm not the bad guy. And I'm strong, and smart, and we're all going to be okay."

He looked at me, his eyes wet, and tried to speak, but only blood bubbled out.

"Kaz, I think we do need to take you somewhere to get patched up. We can stay, or drop you off, or—"

"Anna," Liza said.

I met her gaze in the rear-view mirror. Her expression was of confusion. Upset. Apologetic.

I turned my attention to Kaz. He was smiling, and he'd taken my hand.

"Thank you," he said as blood trickled out of the sides of his mouth. "Thank you for not leaving me."

"Oh," I said as I realized Kaz was no longer alive.

I was glad I hadn't left him to an eternity on the Pickton Farm. Surely there was a better place to spend an afterlife.

He was sitting up now, watching the trees whizz. His face was slashed to ribbons, and his throat was, too. I hadn't noticed the gouge there—the two-centimeter laceration that severed his esophagus, jugular, and all the tendons in his neck, leaving a gaping chasm of death in its wake.

"Just drive," I told Liza.

Kaz's corpse leaned against me, his ghost blissfully unaware of his eternal state.

Chapter Thirty-Two

We drove through the night and the morning, stopping at noon when a notification from Kaz's car dinged, thirsty for fuel. Liza drove an independent station nowhere near any sign of civilization and watched the surroundings for a good fifteen minutes before pulling up to a pump.

"They wouldn't know this quick," I assured her. "What's Empusa gonna do? Tell them all about our demon battle?"

"Turn in your clothes," Liza countered.

"Yeah," I said. "Maybe. But still. They wouldn't come this way so quick."

Maybe, maybe not. But I didn't want Liza to worry. I didn't want anything bad for Liza, not ever again.

"Want food?" I asked.

"I should," she said.

She wasn't hungry. Or couldn't stomach the thought of food after what she'd seen. I can't imagine what it must be like to watch me transform. Knowing demons existed was a hard pill to swallow. I, on the other hand, was ravenous. Like a growing infant, every growth and change beat the piss out of me; I felt like I could devour an entire horse. So, while Liza pumped the gas, I changed into a pair of pants I found in Kaz's trunk, and gave Kaz's ghost a nod to stay put and went inside the gas station.

I didn't feel like chips or chocolate bars. Even the donuts that I used to love so much as a child weren't appealing to me. Thankfully, this gas station was attached to a restaurant, something I didn't notice until I was inside.

I went to the restaurant side and scanned the counter beside the till for a take-away menu.

"Help you, lovey?"

The waitress was rough around the edges, with low-rider jeans exposing the tiger stripes of pregnancy stretch beneath a too-short shirt. The dark circles under her eyes matched the smoky makeup on her eyelids and the crudely drawn cats-eye liner that faded into a smudge. Her teeth were yellow and crooked, accentuated by coral lipstick caked onto her thin lips.

"Do you do take-away?" I asked.

"We can," she said. "I'll toss it in a box for you."

I ordered a couple of turkey sandwiches and a side of fries, even though cold fries in a cardboard container tasted more like soggy paper than the cardboard itself. The waitress scratched the order on a pad and was barking through the window when I noticed a pair of bare feet on the dirty tile floor.

"Be just a few minutes, hon," she said.

I didn't acknowledge the waitress, nor did she wait for an acknowledgment. She was on to the next customer, coffeepot in hand, refilling lukewarm mugs with a fake smile. I was busy looking at the feet, up the set of long legs with two sets of knees, up over the naked torso and breasts, and into the face of Friend.

"Hello, Friend," I said.

She was very different from when we'd met. The first time I saw her, she had no head. And she was dressed in a frilly little bloodstained dress and shiny black patent shoes. Now she was naked, all thin skin and protruding bones, but she sure did have a head, complete with a thick, mangy mane of raven black hair to match her solid black eyes. It was right then that I realized where I was. That same checkered tile floor, same red vinyl booths with that icky, sticking plastic covering

"Can I also get a donut?" I asked the waitress when she sailed past.

"A donut?" she asked.

"A donut," I confirmed.

I took my spot in the very same booth I'd sat in the night Mom and I went on the run after I'd murdered my father. I scootched across the sticky seat, my forearm dragging through some wet remnants left by the previous diners, and looked out the same window into the same dusty parking lot.

"Coffee?" the waitress asked when she deposited my donut in front of me, having to stretch the length of the table.

I nodded. She poured. She left.

I sipped my coffee and nibbled my donut as Friend rounded the corner outside and came to the other side of the window. She pressed her nose against the glass and huffed a breath of hair, fogging up the surface, revealing the ghost of the original design she'd painted there in blood so many moons before. She pressed a finger at the tip of the heart, and I pressed mine on my side of the glass, and together we traced the new design—a tree of hearts, roots encircling it, and crude cave-drawing images of a cardinal, a squirrel, a coyote, and a mystery smudge acting as four corners.

"Anna." Liza slid into the booth across from me.

Like Mom decades before, Liza had the leavings of leftover toilet paper stuck on her face beneath her eyes and under her nose. She'd been crying, and she had tried to clean herself up with toilet paper.

"Want a bite?" I asked.

She shook her head.

"But for sure you'll have some coffee," I said.

I slid my mug over and she took it, cradling it to her face and closing her eyes. She drew a sip. When she lowered the cup, there was blood within, and a blood mustache on her upper lip.

"Want a second cup, ladies?" the waitress asked.

I wasn't sure how long she'd been standing there. But I knew for sure she didn't see the blood in Liza's cup any more than she could see the drawing on the window—one side in donut glaze the other in the black rot of Friend's finger.

"What were you drawing on the window?" Liza asked, her eyes squinted, trying to decipher the design.

"This is the diner," I said. "That night, with Mom."

"What?" she said.

"Yeah," I confirmed.

She looked out the window, her fingers tapping her mug in a nervous staccato. "How did we end up here?" she said. "What does it mean?"

"Everything means something, maybe," I said. "Maybe just happenstance. We're close to Eden."

As if in answer, the window at the neighbouring booth smashed. The scant few customers in the diner yelped and screeched, and everyone stared at the broken window.

"Goddamnit," the waitress said. "Clancy, get the goddamn broom again. Motherfucker."

Clancy, a greying man with grey eyes, skin, and scowl, appeared from the kitchen, dragging a broom behind him. He started sweeping up the glass with as much vigor as a sleeping corpse.

"Again?" I asked the waitress.

"Fourth time this month," she said. "I told the boss man to put some stickers up on that window to stop the birds from flying into it. Window's ain't cheap, and those bird's ain't fuckin' around."

I expected a gull, a raven, or an eagle, a big bird that would carry weight and momentum enough to burst through that window. But when I peered over the booth, it was Erinyes, her red feathers ruffled, her head still absent. I scooped her up into my palms.

"Careful," the waitress said. "You're liable to cut yourself on the glass. Stupid thing's dead, anyway.

Has been for a long time.

Erinyes ruffled her feathers and contorted her body but couldn't tend to the damage without a beak. So I smoothed her feathers for her, plucking out the broken ones and massaging the bent ones back into place.

"Do you see?" I asked Liza.

"I see a dead bird," she said.

Erinyes wriggled out of my grasp and started tearing at my pants with her talons. I tried to pull her off, then shoo her away, but she got increasingly violent, tearing both my clothing and my flesh.

"Stop," I said.

I gave her a solid thwack with the back of my hand, sending her flying off my lap and across the diner floor. After a burst of flapping and hopping around, she took wing and flew straight out of the hole she'd made for herself in the window.

"Fuck," I said, touching my leg where she'd drawn blood.

There was something there. Deep in the pocket of those sweatpants.

"I ain't fucking doin' this no more," Clancy grumbled.

I looked over in time to see the dead bird, all strips of bloody flesh and a broken neck, getting swept into his dustpan. It was a grey jay, and a big one at that. And it did have a head.

"Did you think it was…" Liza paused to recall the name.

"Erinyes?"

"It was her," I said. "On Mom's side of the veil."

I slid my hands into Kaz's pocket and drew out the treasure within. I opened my palm, letting it catch the light which reflected right into my retina, almost blinding me.

"What is it?" Liza asked.

"Fuck," I said. I rolled it around in my hand, studied it, not believing what I was seeing. "Fuck," I repeated as I brought it up on the table and held it out to Liza.

After the events of the past week, there wasn't much of Liza's golden colour left in her face, but what was there drained, leaving the paste of grey ivory behind.

"Fuck," she said, and her lower lip began to tremble.

"I took it," I said, remembering my hand closing around the crystal in the master bedroom of that horrible trailer. "I held it," as I battled Empusa and saved Kaz's body. "I tucked it into the pants after I put them on," I said, aware of every bit of the rough fabric on my legs and torso.

Liza spoke a single word, cut-off and punctuated by a sob. "Mary."

And there it was, on the table between us, the bloodstone Mary used to carry everywhere with her. She carried it all the way to the Pickton Farm, where I was meant to find it.

"I was right," I said. "We have to go back."

"Back?"

I picked up the crystal and held it tight in my fist. It throbbed with the heat and blood of my heartbeat, but also with a pulse of its own. "Eden's Edge."

Chapter Thirty-Three

We didn't know the way. And how could we? The last time I came here from the diner was decades ago, and I was focused on the little headless girl holding a bowl of blood in the seat next to me. Liza didn't know the way, either. She'd been asleep on the journey to Eden's Edge, in the back seat of Allison's SUV as her dad watched out the window at the forest whizzing by. But we didn't need to know the way.

Once we left the diner and pulled out of the parking lot in the direction, I remembered us going all those years ago, I had Liza stop on the shoulder. She waited in the car as I walked into the ditch, just past the treeline, and fell to my knees. I plunged my hands into the dirt, closed my eyes, and brought fistfuls of soil to my face, eating it in clumps until the sensation of worms wriggled in my veins and mud sloshed in my organs. I opened my eyes and blinked away loam, then returned to the car.

Liza drove again in the direction I pointed. We were silent, save the raspy bubbles popping in Kaz's neck wound, but Liza didn't hear it, so I didn't mind as much. She also didn't see that the car was occupied to max capacity—her and me in the front, and Kaz, Friend, and Trebor in the backseat. Kaz was squished in the middle, leaving Friend and Trebor gazing out their windows, with their respective bowls of fluid balanced in their laps. Her bowl was blood, his was tears.

We drove in silence, save the splishing of the liquid in the bowls when we bumped over potholes and the thudding of Kaz's body in the boot. We drove until dusk and the forest was a silhouette against the red sky.

It wasn't a terribly far drive. We followed the highway—first pavement, then gravel. I switched on the radio, remembering that Eden's Edge was tucked off the highway about four songs deeps down a narrow gravel road.

'EDEN'S EDGE' the sign declared.

But I didn't need a sign to know we'd arrived. The place was as familiar as Mom's touch.

"Wow," Liza said as we curved with the road, rolling to a stop at the spot where Allison's house used to stand. Now it was ash and rot, a vine-covered concrete hole of a basement exposed to the air.

I was glad Liza couldn't see behind my veils. Because I wouldn't want anyone, especially her, seeing Laz still hanging there, covered in his filth, head lolled to the side.

I looked away.

"What is it?"

She didn't prod when I didn't answer.

We parked the car and got out. I opened the back doors wide and left them gaping. An invitation for everyone to join, even though I wasn't sure they would.

"Where are we go—"

But I was already moving. I wanted to tell Liza not to follow me, to stay in the car, but I wasn't sure she'd be safe in the car. Or anywhere. She could decide what safety was or wasn't and whether she wanted the risk.

I made my way around the perimeter of the compound, ensuring that I didn't glance across the green space that I'd murdered—all the houses that I'd burnt down, all the bodies that melted within. I hadn't killed them, but I hadn't freed them either. I hoped that they'd moved on. No one deserved to live their days stuck in Eden's Edge.

I reached the trees and entered the thick brush. There was no path. No one had been here in decades. The canopy of tree branches overheard were like fingers tented together, and I expected to see the Blankness—my dad, Khuya. He'd visited me many times on this very path before I knew who the creature was. But he was no longer there. It made me worry that Mom wouldn't be in our yard, either. I would go back and check, but first, the cemetery.

It was exactly as I'd remembered it. The graves were only slightly overgrown, and the lichgate still stood. Even the tops of the headstones appeared to have been wiped clean, and I thought of Mary bouncing through this mini field of the dead, wiping off headstones while her curls sproinged off her shoulders.

Trebor and Friend were there, lingering at the edge of the woods with Gus on her shoulder and Erinyes in the trees above. I left them where they were. They were there if I needed them.

The brush to my left rustled, and mice, bitty birds, and skittering insects scattered.

"Hello?" I said.

A crack rang through the woods—the snap of a branch breaking under someone's weight.

"It's me," I said. "Anna."

He appeared from the bush like a specter, all rotting and deformed, sporting a single yellow logan on his right foot and a Nor 'Wester' atop his massive skull. He saw me and gasped. Drool poured from his throat over the spout where his tongue and lower jaw used to be.

"Old Man Merle," I said, my voice cracking when I smiled.

His gaze moved over my body, his head cocked, trying to determine whether I was speaking the truth about who I was. He must have decided it was me, because he loped towards me in four galloping strides, picking me up and whirling me around while laughter and garbled speech leaked from his throat.

"Gahhhh gahhhh gahhhh gahhhh!"

"I'm happy to see you, too," I said.

And I was. Old Man Merle was happiness, a bright yellow sunshine in this storm of a place. I held his hands, and we looked at each other, both of us smiling and weeping. His face scrunched in worry when Friend and Trebor flanked me, Trebor being twice the height and width of the old ghoul of a fisherman.

"It's okay," I told Merle. "They're my friends. Well, actually…they're me."

Trebor bowed his head in a nod and his cock-snakes quivered a wave. Merle recoiled and crunched his nose in disgust, then Friend stepped forward. She curtsied, and he bowed, and they embraced. He didn't whirl her around like he did me, but I think her appearance was a bit off-putting, what with all those knees and elbows. And besides, he'd never seen her with a head.

"How have you been, Merle?" I asked.

"Gahhhh," he said.

"Ah. Well, you're probably wondering why I'm back," I said.

Old Man Merle knocked the wind out of me when he picked me up and whirled me around again. I laughed, and he cried and moaned until we were both crying again and he put me down.

"Yes, yes, Merle," I said. "I'm glad to be back. Sorry it took me so long."

Merle sniffled, then looked down the path from where I'd come. The darkening of his expression told me he had information that I wanted.

"Who's here, Merle?"

His worried expression turned to fear, and he lifted an elongated, crooked finger to point into the trees.

"How many?" I asked.

He held up his two hands, a peace sign on each.

"Four people?"

"Gahhhh," he said with a shrug. He dropped a single finger.

"Three people," I said. "And one…something else."

"Gahhhh," he said with a nod.

Empusa.

I wanted to ask him about the people. Who they were, how big they were, if they had weapons. But I supposed that didn't matter. I was a weapon, and Empusa was likely the only one I had to worry about.

"Anna." Liza burst out of the woods, and her voice was a whisper.

I looked behind her, expecting she was being chased.

"There's someone here," she said.

"I know," I said.

"Besides…" She waved a hand over the cemetery. She knew I wasn't alone here, even though she only saw me and not my many companions.

"I know," I repeated. "Who?"

"Don't know," she said. "But there are tents. And a fire. And I heard people talking."

"Where are the tents?"

Liza bit her lower lip.

"Mom's house," I said. Of course. Whoever this was came here because of me. They led me here, so where else would they set up camp? "I want you to go to the car," I said. "Stay there. Lock the doors."

"No—"

"Yes." When I spoke, the word cut the air like a sword, a trio of voices full of heaven and hell.

"Anna, I …" Liza cupped my face and kissed me, pushing her tongue into my mouth. Her tears were salty, and mine were too, and we cried into each other in a tangle of limbs, hair, and tears.

When we pulled apart, connected by a thin web of drool, she breathed words into my mouth. "I love you."

"I love you," I replied.

Giggles.

Old Man Merle, Friend, and Trebor were standing side by side amongst the graves, holding hands, shit-eating grins on their faces. I kissed Liza one more time, and they cooed, awed, and blinked lovey eyes. Old Man Merle stood tall like a proud grandfather. He hugged the two of us together, but Liza took no noticed. I did hope she felt it in her heart.

"I'll lead the way," I said.

And I did. It was easy to find my way back to Eden's Edge. The land beyond the trees was flickering with the orange of flame that licked through the trees as ash rained onto my hair. But nothing was burning. Nothing but maybe a campfire that was keeping these intruders warm. This was just the flames of hell that'd I'd been chasing since I left Vancouver, running towards my past and my future.

When we reached the clearing of the compound, I nodded in the direction opposite of Mom's house, back towards the car. Liza conceded and left. She didn't look back, but I knew there were tears streaming down her cheeks. Liza's tears were searing creeks down my face. And though my own crying had ceased, Friend was still bawling, her frail body wracked with sobs.

Eden was burning. Fires beyond the veil roared clear across what was a swath of homes, yards, and gardens. The aroma of scorched wood and the stench of cooking meat hung in the air like fog as I found the lane. I walked, my head held high, reminiscing as I passed the remains of places I once knew: the Beast, the foster home, Library House. Nothing here but ash. Not even ghosts. This warmed my heart. They'd all gone. No one was stuck here.

Well. Maybe not no one.

Mom's house wasn't standing, but the yard was. It was still encircled by dead cardinals, their bodies as fat, fresh, and crimson as the day they died. There were, indeed, some tents erected in the grass, made of cheap blue tarps and branches from the woods. And in the center of the yard was the throne Old Man Merle had made for me, the moose rack mounted on the top.

And on that throne sat a sickly woman. She was small and thin, with skin like worn leather and only a few rotted teeth in her mouth. Below her stained yellow tank top sagged a pair of deflated breasts resting on a concave stomach. Low rider jeans revealed a mangled mess of pubic hair that squeezed overtop the denim. Even at a distance, beyond the ring of cardinals, the damage life had done was visible on her body: scars on her face, track marks on her inner arms, a tremor in both hands, and a manic-tapping foot.

I stepped over the ring of birds, not slowing until I stood in front of this derelict Queen of Eden. Her head tilted, and her greasy ringlets stuck to the side of her face as Empusa stepped up beside her and rested a hand on the throne.

"Hello Mary," I said.

Chapter Thirty-Four

"Hello Anna."

Mary had aged. Her face was all scars and wrinkles, as was her body, but I'd recognise those curls, that button nose, and those smoky green eyes anywhere. I'd been sad at the thought of Mary trapped out here, spending her eternity in the place where she'd been tortured, assaulted, and murdered. But she didn't die here. She didn't die at all.

Mary was no ghost. She was living, breathing, flesh and blood.

"Mary," I said. I was going to ask her how she'd been, but, well…

"Nice of you to come back," she said.

"You expected it," I said. An observation, not a question.

"I invited you," she said.

"It was you," I said, by gaze flickering from her to Empusa and back.

"What was me?" Mary asked.

"The bodies," I said. "The dumpster, the grocery store, the

apartment above mine. The farm."

She giggled. The strained, frantic tone of her once joyful voice told me this was no longer the Mary I once knew.

"Sure did," she said as she twirled a ringlet around her finger.

"How?" I asked.

Mary was small and sickly. An addict of some sort—the victim of abuse who'd never recovered.

"I had help," she said as she gestured to Empusa.

"Where'd you two meet?" I asked.

"At the farm," Mary said. "After Bobby took me there, but not before he fucked my gash open from bellybutton to tailbone."

She uncrossed her legs, revealing mess of a vulva that looked like it had been torn, repaired, and reconstructed a great many times. It was all bruises and scars, stretched, limp, and deformed.

"Don't like it?" she said as she licked her lips.

"I don't like it for you," I said. "I don't like what happened to you."

"You don't fucking care," she sneered. "You let me go."

"What?" I said.

"You saw me," she said. She stood from the throne and staggered forward as bottles of liquor fell from her lap onto the ground. "That night," she said, slurring and stumbling towards me, her finger stabbing the air in my direction. "That night that Bobby put his fingers in me, beat me, and shoved me in the back of the car. You watched me, your eyes on mine, as they drove away. And do you know what he did, Anna? Do you know what he did to me at that farm?"

I shook my head. I had words, but they were lodged like a stone in my throat.

"You can imagine," she said. "Because you're evil, just like him. Just like all the evil fucks that hurt, take, rape, and eat."

Empusa was moving with Mary, a step behind her.

"When did Empusa come?" I asked.

"After Bobby beat the baby out of me with the blunt end of his pitchfork," Mary said. "Don't know why he was so mad at that li'l fetus. He's the one put it there, after all."

"She was there after you miscarried?" I asked.

"I miscarried *her*," Mary said, looking lovingly at her demon familiar. More than a rider but attached just the same.

"It's been so many years," I said. "What do you want from me?"

"What do I want?" Mary said, her voice increasing in volume and pitch. "What do I *want*? I want you to *suffer*!"

Two young women made of skin, bone, and devastation, just like Mary, crawled out of a tent, filthy bras and panties covering damaged flesh.

"Do you know how long we were at that farm, Anna? Locked in that barn, drinking animal piss and eating shit to stay alive? All while bleeding from our asses, pussies, and mouths? He destroyed us, but you left us to die!"

"How was I supposed to—"

"You looked right at me, Anna. Right into my motherfucking eyes when he took me to die!"

All those bodies, their eyes missing.

"See me now, cunt?" Mary screamed, and spittle flew from her mouth.

She was too far gone—a marionette, and Empusa held the strings. With all that abuse and trauma, Mary had dedicated her life to blame and revenge. And every bit of it was aimed at me.

"You came here," she said, "And evil befell this place, then you left, Anna. You abandoned every bit of us, and you went about your pretty little life like we'd never existed!"

I couldn't argue with her. All of that was true, whether I was at fault or not.

"Mary?"

No!

Liza was behind me. I didn't want her there. I wanted her in the car, driving far, far away. I wished I could boost her like I did out of that basement window, and that she would run away, through the woods, into a different life, a different world, where there were no demons, witches, pain, nor me.

"And *you*," Mary said. "Shacking up with this cunt. How *dare* you live your life like mine meant *nothing*!"

She picked up a rock and hurled it at Liza's head. My skin burst, and my talon thrust out, catching the rock before it made contact. Mary was startled. The whites of her eyes glowed in the dark. Empusa stepped forward as Mary backed up, and the two women behind Mary came to her side.

"You're a beast," Mary spat. "Always were."

"Yes," I agreed.

I am.

"We escaped," she said, motioning to the other women. "Empusa helped us, and we worked together to frame you. To make you see, to have them lock you up forever like you meant for us to be."

"Do it," Liza whispered.

She wanted me to change, to slaughter the lot of them.

"If I take out Empusa," I said, "maybe I can save Mary."

Like I should have saved her.

"But Bobby," Liza said. "He died when his rider did."

"He was a bad man," I said. "And I killed both his rider and him. If I just take out Empusa…"

The time for discussion was over. The two other women lunged forward and snatched Liza while Mary sat back on the throne. Empusa was meant to take care of me. I would deal with her after I made sure Liza was safe. I swung my arm to swipe the women with my talons, but Empusa grabbed me by the wrist, stopping me.

There was nothing I could do. The two Pickton victims were pulling Liza away; one had her by the hair and the other was struggling to keep a hold of her wrists. I screamed, and the earth beneath my feet trembled.

"Very scary," Empusa said. "But get a load of this."

Empusa's hair ignited into a halo of fire as she pointed at me with her mantis-swords for arms, her donkey leg pawing the ground to tell me she was going to charge.

"You speak in tongues, you hear the voices, you manifest your change," Empusa said. "Like you spoke to me in Greek in that hospital, in Latin in that church."

I am demon, I am witch...

"I am daimones, just like yourself," Empusa said. "So, show me what you got, little girrrrrrl."

I focused on my dad—all the times he yelled, smashed stuff, the look on his face when I sliced him open, and his life bled to the ground. With every memory, my body cracked, shifted, reformed until I was the demon within—tall, thick, and dark. Trebor stood behind me, still towering as he pressed against me and entered me from behind, his cocks filling all the voids in my body and propelling me forward.

But I resisted moving towards Empusa. I tried to kneel, but she leapt through the air, landing in front of me and shattering my teeth with an uppercut to my lower jaw. It didn't hurt—it was more noise than pain—but before I could regain my senses, she had me in a headlock, twisting me to face Liza and the women who were trying to tear her apart.

"You got eyes, bitch," Mary said. "You watched me being taken away to my death, and now you'll watch hers."

I was going to scream to rid my mind of its agony, but Empusa thrust a fist into my mouth, bottling in all my pain. Liza was putting up a good fight, but it was two against one. That may not have been a problem because these women were sickly and frail, but Mary was walking towards her with a Bowie knife in her hand.

I wanted to tell her no. Plead with her to stop. Beg her to remember our brief time together as children and that we were still her friends. But Empusa was filling my mouth and pinning my body between a brass thigh and a muscular donkey leg. Mary held the tip of the knife out. It caught the gleam of the moon as it poked Liza in the throat. Liza dropped to the ground, evading death, but the women were on top of her like hyenas, pinning her arms and legs while Mary straddled her hips.

"You want to feel me inside you?" Mary asked as she slid the knife up Liza's belly, between her breasts, and stopping at her throat.

Liza wasn't struggling anymore. Her tears dripped into the dirt beneath her head.

Fight, I wanted to scream, but Empusa held tight. I writhed in her grasp but couldn't budge a centimeter.

Mary placed her other hand on the knife, wrapping both around the hilt, preparing to drive it in when a woman fell to the side, freeing Liza's arm.

"What the fuck?" Mary yelled at the woman.

She was slapping and clawing at her legs and warbling a painful sound.

The other woman fell, crawling away from Liza and ripping at her flesh. Liza took the opportunity to buck her hips, sending Mary off balance and crashing into the ground.

"You fucking whores," Mary shrieked. "What the hell is wrong with you?"

"It burns," one of the women yelled.

"Get them off," the other one screeched.

I studied their legs. They were covered in dirt from kneeling on the ground beside Liza. That's what I thought until the dirt moved. It wasn't soil, mud, or leaves. Their legs were covered in fire ants. The women were scratching and slapping, but there were so many ants covering their legs, crawling up their shorts and shirts, and one was wiping ants out of her eyes.

Liza took the opportunity. She pulled a screwdriver out of

her back pocket, tackled one of the women, and stabbed the screwdriver through her eye socket. The woman was quiet—peaceful, almost—as she fell to the ground twitching, her fingers playing a distant piano as her life slipped away. Liza didn't watch this beautiful but grotesque display of death. She was already on top of the other woman, slashing a smile across her throat from ear to ear with a box cutter she must have also had in her pocket. That death wasn't quiet. The woman grabbed her throat with her hands as blood poured out, and she wailed, spraying blood in mist into the air. It took her a solid minute to stop moving and making such wretched noises.

"There was nothing we could do," Liza said to the ground.

She was talking to Mary.

I used my razor-sharp teeth to bite into Empusa. Bone cracked beneath the force of my jaws. She yanked her arms away. I did a half-pirouette, swinging wildly and slashing her flesh into ribbons with my talons. I hooked my leg around the back of her brass knee and took her to the ground before stomping her forehead with my foot. Her eyes rolled, and her head lolled to the side, but she wasn't gone. Not yet.

"Liza," I said. "Don't."

She had almost reached Mary with a third weapon—the four-headed goat wine stopper. She had a hold of it by the goats with the sharp end pointed at Mary.

"She's going to kill us," Liza said. "She was trying to ruin you."

"But she didn't," I said. "And only because she's broken, Liza. This is it. This is my chance to save her."

Liza hesitated. It was all the pause Mary needed to swing that Bowie knife through the air.

I had heard about traumatic events, and how everything falls into slow motion. I never believed it until that moment when it happened. I didn't run for Liza or Mary, and I didn't yell or throw something to misdirect the blow. I dropped to my knees and plunged my talons into the dirt until I was elbow deep, the tips of my claws scraping rock and clay. Then I smashed my face into the soil, breathing it into my lungs, welcoming it into my body.

A wave of heat blew me out of the dirt and onto my haunches. I was poised to attack, but I was awestruck by the ring of fire surrounding us. The cardinals, once dead, were now crimson flames, their wings flapping smoke and fire over the yard. Erinyes landed on Empusa, causing her flesh to sizzle and blister as Gus attacked her face, popping her eyeballs with his incisors.

"Take her," I screamed at Liza. "Out of the ring!"

She opened her mouth, an argument on her tongue, but the cardinals erupted into a choral climax, the noise ethereal and deafening.

Liza was dragging Mary by the hair out of the yard.

I turned to Empusa.

"How?" she screeched. "I'm an old daimones, and powerful! You cannot defeat me!"

"I am something you aren't," I said.

I walked to her while thinking of Mom—red feathers and lavender tea. The feel of a paperback novel in my hand. Fresh vegetables from the garden and the haunting melody of a bow dancing across cello strings. My body shrank, forming back into a woman, soft, smart, and strong.

"I am demon, I am witch …" I said, my voice an ancient lilt.

Empusa fell to her knees as Erinyes beat her with razor-sharp wings, and Gus clawed at her throat.

"Half-breed tainted rotten bitch!" I said.

I bit through Empusa's throat, taking a good chunk of meat into my mouth and swallowing it before going back for more. Trebor and Friend joined me. Soon all of us, bird and squirrel included, had picked Empusa's bones clean. I left it to Trebor and Friend to grind her bones to fertilizer for the flowers.

Chapter Thirty-Five

"Liza."

The fires had been doused by a sudden onslaught of damp, moist air. The yard was back to normal, with a ring of bird bones as a perimeter. I ran into the front yard, or the place where the front yard had once been, and found Liza standing a few meters from Mary's body.

"Is she dead?" I asked.

Liza shook her head.

Mary's chest rose and fell. I knelt beside her and wiped her sweaty, greasy hair from her face. Her gaze was fixed, her eyes looking somewhere past me, straight through me, and tendrils of drool were dribbling out of her moving mouth.

"She's trying to speak," I said.

I lowered my ear to her mouth to listen to garbled whispers and nonsensical language, all air and monotone song.

"She's gone," Liza said.

"She's not dead," I said.

"But what?" Liza asked. "She's what now? Brain dead?"

I wasn't sure what effect killing a rider would have on their host. Especially Empusa, who was both rider and familiar, a spawn of trauma. But the evil was dead, and I hoped it had left the girl behind. At least some of her.

"We can't leave her," I said. "I won't. Not again."

Liza nodded. "But what are we going to do?"

We had no options. If we went for medical care, they'd nab me for the murders. If we didn't, Mary and Kaz would die. And I couldn't expect Liza to spend the rest of her life on the lam.

Friend stood by us but Trebor stayed back, pounding Empusa's bone dust into the dirt.

"I know," I said.

I had no energy left. My body had been used, roughed up, broken, and repaired, but still I ran. There were no structures left in Eden's Edge except one, so I was able to cut across the whole property in a straight line to get to my destination.

So much had changed. I slowed to a walk when I reached Friend's house. There were familiar things, like the two bowls set atop pillars on either side of the top step. The house was still crooked, with the roof perched on the structure like a crumpled hat. The wood walls were bowed this way and that, and each board was painted a different colour, though those colours were much more muted than when I had seen them all those years ago. I still imagined it would be quite the sight in the sunlight. And the base of the house wasn't made of shiny, black shoes filled by bloated feet and crumpled like a mattress compressed beneath a great weight. The child feet were gone, replaced by women's feet—high heels, blisters, callouses, precisely manicured toenails.

I went up the front step and tried the door. Still locked.

"May I go in?" I said to Friend, who was standing next to me on the porch.

She embraced me, her arms and legs locking around me as she gargled a song deep in her throat.

"I'd like to live here," I said. "We could all be safe here, right?"

Friend kissed me on the neck, then a peck on the lips, leaving a tacky string of black rot between us as she jerked and jittered to the door, placed her hand on the knob, and slipped inside.

I wasn't yet invited in.

I returned to Liza and Mary, sat in the dirt and cried, knowing what I needed to do.

Chapter Thirty-Six

Beep. Beep. Beep.

Hissssss.

A moan somewhere in the distance down a hallway illuminated by spastic fluorescent lighting.

I hated hospitals.

But Mary was here, hooked up to IVs and machines, and she was going to be almost fine.

Except for the brain trauma, that is.

Liza sat looking out the window, waiting. I was waiting, too, to hear the sirens that would reach my ears before the red and blue light ever reached her eyes.

"They're here," she said.

I hadn't heard a thing. "I didn't hear sirens," I said.

"And they don't have their lights on," she said.

Odd.

It seemed like an eternity before there was a knock at the hospital door.

"Come in," I said, as if they needed my permission.

Kaz entered first. I tried not to react, but I was equal parts terrified and elated to see him. He was still wearing his blood-soaked shirt and that wicked quartet of slashes across his throat and face, but he was smiling, even though he was very, very dead.

Behind him came two detectives, a man and a woman, neither smelling like a donkey and both having human legs.

"Anna Eden?" the female officer asked.

I raised my hand like a terrified schoolgirl.

"You've had quite the exciting few weeks, it seems," she said.

"My life is a circus," I said. "I don't see how it's fair I have no monkeys."

Both officers laughed. They weren't tense, angry, nor accusatory in any way.

"There's a lot to sift through here, what with the trail of bodies," the woman said, "but detective Kaziel left us some pretty comprehensive notes. So let me say, first off, I apologize for your incarceration and the department's mishandling of these cases."

What?

The officers gave me the Coles Notes version. Or I was so shocked I condensed it in my mind as I heard the details.

Empusa. Holding Mary and the other women captive at the Pickton Farm. Mary and her mates had left evidence all over those bodies—hair, fingerprints, saliva. Empusa had fingered me. But Empusa helped me break out, intent on framing and killing me and making it look like a procedural kill. And when we called the police from the radio in Kaz's car at Eden's Edge, and they sent the cavalry to retrieve us, they found a swath of victims, and nothing more.

"All that after what you went through with Allison and Robert," the female cop said.

"I'd rather not talk about that," I said.

The male cop was going to open his mouth and say something, but the female cop held up her hand. "We will not be causing you any more anguish. In fact, our legal department would like to ensure that your trauma, and our handling of these cases, does not result in lasting consequences for you. I know they are drafting a proposed settlement—"

I didn't hear the rest of it. I didn't care. We were free. And it was terrifying. The world was a big place, and I was responsible for more than myself now. The love in her eyes told me that I was stuck with Liza for the long haul, and the thought sent ripples of warmth through my body, brain, and hearts. And Mary…

I'd never let her down again.

"We'll discuss all of this," Liza said, "once things settle down."

"Of course," the female officer said. "Like I said, the department will meet with Miss Eden next week to finalize the compensation, if she agrees to it. In the meantime, we are happy to put you up in our department housing while you get back on your feet. We have a house for transient witness relocation, and you can stay there for up to four months."

More things were said. I heard very little. The cops thanked us, patted me on the back, and left.

Mary's machines beeped and hissed.

Liza held my hand. "What do you want to do?" she asked.

"Process all of this."

"Do you want… I can go home. To my apartment."

"Do you want that?" I asked.

"Absolutely not."

"We can't go to mine," I said. "We should take them up on that house offer. We'll need the space for…"

I looked over at Mary, at her vacant eyes and limp limbs. She'd need special equipment, space for a wheelchair, a yard to sit in and enjoy the childhood she'd lost.

"It's ours," Liza said.

"What's ours?"

"You didn't hear?" she asked.

No. I didn't.

"Eden," she said. "That piece of land was surrendered to the precinct back when it burned down. It was legally Allison's, and she left no one behind, but records show you as the last known occupant. It deferred to you."

What?

"Eden's Edge?" I asked.

"Yeah," Liza said, her lip trembling in both joy and sorrow.

"I own it?" I said, my breath hitching in my throat.

"Yep," Liza concerned, a sob escaping with the word.

It was too much. My mind could hardly bear the consequences, the possibilities. So much good was in Eden, and so much evil. The laughter of children and the screams of slaughter. Gardens and ash, Old Man Merle and Bobby Pickton. It was both glorious and horrid.

Just like me.

Epilogue 491

Wind rustled through the trees, carrying the sweet smell of decaying autumn leaves and fermenting apples. Gus frolicked in the piles of deadfall, sending sprays of red, gold, and orange leaves into the air. Erinyes was fluffed into a feather ball neck deep in the birdbath that I'd just filled with warm water from the kettle. Old Man Merle was smoking a pipe, watching the clouds roll across the sky as he lounged in the Adirondack chair I built for him as thanks for my throne.

Liza appeared beside me with a pitcher of strawberry lemonade. "Such a lovely day," she said. She sat beside me on the porch swing overlooking the yard and rocked. We held hands, and she rested her head on my shoulder. "I'm thinking I'll paint the basement tomorrow," she said.

"What colour?"

"Not sure," she said. "Want to run to the store with me later and look at some paint swatches? We can stop for some Tim Hortons on the way back."

Mary's head slowly faced us.

"Yes," I said to Mary. "We'll grab you a honey cruller."

She smiled, then let her head fall back to the side as she slumped in her wheelchair. She loved to be wheeled to the edge of the porch to watch the clouds roll by. I often felt like she could see Erinyes and Gus play. Once, I think I heard the tiniest giggle come from somewhere deep in her belly. But I didn't know for sure. It had been a year, and she still hadn't spoken, could barely move on her own. We fed her blended food and changed her diapers, washed and styled her ringlets, which were back to the strawberry blonde shimmer they'd once been.

Would death have been better?

Perhaps I did it for me. For my guilty conscious. But moments like these, joy at the mention of a donut, erased any regret that simmered below my surface.

I didn't know what life would hold now. We had money, we'd built a beautiful house on Mom's lot in Eden's Edge, and I had the love of my life at my side. I could live out my days like this, full of peace, joy, and beauty.

I could do all that and not be bothered if it wasn't for the small changes.

A glance in the mirror to find a red feather sprouting from my chin.

The random loss of a blackened molar in an otherwise healthy mouth.

The darkening and loss of all my nails.

One eye turned solid black, the other, glacial blue.

And at night, beneath the gentle whir of Mary's oxygen in the next room and the soft purr of Liza's snores on the pillow beside mine, was a song sang by two voices, high and low, a dissonant duet.

Witch and demon,
gossamer and pitch,
half breed, tainted, rotten bitch.

About the Author

Jae Mazer is a Canadian who was born in Victoria, British Columbia, and grew up in the prairies of Northern Alberta. After spending the majority of her life battling sasquatches in the Great White North, she migrated south to Texas to have a go at the armadillos. She is a connoisseur and creator of gothic horror, splatterfolk, splatter westerns, and folk horror. She's degreed, won awards, been in anthologies, has chameleon hair and lots of skin ink, and enjoys mustard and alcohol.

Awards:

- ATAI 2017, WINNER, Best Horror Novel for *Chrysalis and Clan*
- American Book Fest 2019, Best Horror Novel for *Crone: A Witch's Tale*

- Next Generation Indie Book Awards 2019 Runner-up/Finalist for *Crone: A Witch's Tale*
- Next Generation Indie Book Awards 2021 Runner-up/Finalist for *Blood Wail.*
- New York City Midnight Finalist for Short Screenplay for *Just Like Momma*

OTHER HELLBOUND BOOKS

The First Time I Saw Her

Anna and her mother are on the run after a tragedy shatters their world. A stranger has offered them protection in a private community hidden deep in the woods, and Anna and her mother have no choice but to abandon their life and belongings to take refuge until they can figure out their next move.

But the woman who helped them may not be what she seems, and the safe-haven community has its own secrets ... and its own dangers.

Anna is no ordinary girl, though. She can perceive things others cannot, impossible things. Now thrust into an unfamiliar setting with horrors unfolding all around her, Anna must figure out what she is and what she is capable of before she loses what little she has left of her life.

THE FIRST TIME I SAW HER is the first installment in the Gossamer and Pitch Trilogy, a series about love and hate, witches and demons, and the sheer veil between life and death.

The Black Monastery
(Translated from its Native Hungarian)

1866. Corpus Christi, Texas.

This deeply devout Catholic small town, still reeling from the wounds of war, has barely begun to recover when it faces yet another calamity.
Under the cover of night, unknown assailants brutally murder local priests and abduct altar boys. Even the Saint Lucia Nunnery on the outskirts of town isn't spared by the merciless perpetrators.

Aisztid Wratiszlaw, the town's Hungarian-born sheriff, is left with only one blood-stained message on the chapel wall:

"Without the shedding of blood, there is no forgiveness of sins!"

As the sheriff and his misfit posse set out to hunt down the brutal cult, but their mission is hindered not only by the tensions within their group but also by their living nightmares: Terrifying biblical stories brought to life before their very eyes and the haunting question of whether they're facing more than mere mortals this time…

Satan Rides Your Daughter Again

Welcome to the second volume of HellBound's satanic-themed anthology, our homage to all things Old Nick and those who worship him and his demonic underlings!

From a poor woman suffering at the hands of witch finders, the building of an infamous Bunny Ranch and absolute living Hell that is high school, to encounters with angels, Hades' pit, the quest for a hellishly good chilli, and so much more in between, Satan Rides Your Daughter Again is packed with devilishly good tales to torment your soul with a taste of the fire and brimstone underworld that roils below us…

Featuring some of the very best independent horror authors committing words to paper today: R.D. Tyler, Dan Bolden, K A Douglas, Dylan Bosworth, Conor O'Brian Barnes, Dan Muenzer, Josh Darling, Barend Nieuwstraten III, Matthew Fryer, Kevin L. Kennel, J Louis Messina, Terry Grimwood, James Musgrave, Donn L. Hess, Shannon Lawrence, Chase Hughes, KT Bartlett, Sarah Goodman, Mariah Southworth, and Terry Campbell.

Notes Of Discord

These Squatters Are Going To Rot! In the late eighties, the Lower East Side of New York City rippled with turmoil. It was the city against the poor and destitute, it was punk versus skin versus hippy. All of it had a soundtrack, call it drunk punk, call it what you would, the LES throbbed with a new generation of punkers pushing the boundaries. Underneath it lay an evil that even the headline writers of the Post could never have imagined. An unearthly evil that twists the will, an evil that an up and coming punk band will never forget. An evil that will never forget them.

Notes of Discord, part coming of age story, part personal memoir, and all horror novel. A book with lots of punk rock, and even more full-on bloody bits.

The Horror Writer

"The most definitive guide into the trials and tribulations of being a horror writer since Stephen King's 'On Writing.'"

We have assembled some of the very best in the business from whom you can learn so much about the craft of horror writing: Bram Stoker Award© winners, bestselling authors, a President of the Horror Writers' Association, and myriad contemporary horror authors of distinction.

The Horror Writer covers how to connect with your market and carve out a sustainable niche in the independent horror genre, how to tackle the writer's ever-lurking nemesis of productivity, writing good horror stories with powerful, effective scenes, realistic, flowing dialogue and relatable characters without resorting to clichéd jump scares and well-worn gimmicks. Also covered is the delicate subject of handling rejection with good grace, and how to use those inevitable "not quite the right fit for us at this time" letters as an opportunity to hone your craft. Plus... perceptive interviews to provide an intimate peek into the psyche of the horror author and the challenges they work through to bring their nefarious ideas to the page.

And, as if that – and so much more – was not enough, we have for your delectation Ramsey Campbell's beautifully insightful analysis of the tales of HP Lovecraft.

Featuring:

Ramsey Campbell, John Palisano, Chad Lutzke, Lisa Morton, Kenneth W. Cain, Kevin J. Kennedy, Monique Snyman, Scott Nicholson, Lucy A. Snyder, Richard Thomas, Gene O'Neill, Jess Landry, Luke Walker, Stephanie M. Wytovich, Marie O'Regan, Armand Rosamilia, Kevin Lucia, Ben Eads, Kelli Owen, Jasper Bark, and Bret McCormick.

And interviews with: Steve Rasnic Tem, Stephen Graham Jones, David Owain Hughes, Tim Waggoner, and Mort Castle.

A HellBound Books LLC
Publication

www.hellboundbooks.com

SIGN UP FOR THE HELLBOUND BOOKS NEWSLETTER:

Printed in the United States of America